T H E   B O

STIR-FRY
DISHES

T H E · B O O K · O F

STIR-FRY
DISHES

ELIZABETH WOLF-COHEN

Photographed by
KEN FIELD

HPBooks

ANOTHER BEST SELLING VOLUME FROM HPBOOKS

HPBooks
Published by The Berkley Publishing Group
200 Madison Avenue
New York, NY 10016

9 8 7 6

ISBN 1-55788-085-9

By arrangement with Salamander Books Ltd.

Home Economists: Kerenza Harries and Jo Craig
Printed and bound in Spain

CONTENTS

INTRODUCTION

The wok is one of the most versatile pieces of kitchen equipment, it's quick to use, easy to take care of, and perfect for cooking everything from meat, fish and vegetables to pasta and fruit.

Although it's been in use for thousands of years in China, the wok is still ideal for modern cooking with its emphasis on healthy eating. In a wok, food is cooked quickly and lightly at a very high temperature. This seals in all the flavor and helps to retain the texture and color as well as essential nutrients.

This book has over 100 delicious recipes for cooking in the wok, including ones for fish, poultry, meat, vegetables, fruit, pasta, rice and noodles. Each recipe is illustrated in full color and with step-by-step instructions, making this the perfect book for anyone who enjoys good food fast and with the minimum of fuss.

COOKING IN A WOK

The wok was probably invented by the ancient Chinese as a response to the constant fuel shortage. It is still the all-purpose cooking utensil in Southeast Asia, but the recent popularity of regional Chinese, Thai, Vietnamese and Malay cuisines has made it indispensable in Western kitchens as well. The wok's round bottom and high sloping side conduct heat more evenly than other cookware, so food stirred over a high heat cooks quickly, retaining bright color, fresh flavor, vitamins and nutrients. This quick-cooking method is also economical. Although lean, tender cuts of meat are required, a little goes a long way, as they are often cooked with several kinds of vegetables. Because a very small amount of oil or fat is required, stir-fried food is generally low in fat, cholesterol and calories.

Although stir-frying is quick and easy, preparation of ingredients is very important and every one must be prepared before cooking begins. To ensure food cooks quickly and evenly, cut or chop all ingredients into relatively small, evenly shaped pieces.

CHOOSING A WOK

The traditional, inexpensive Chinese wok is probably still the best. Carbon steel, the best conductor of heat, is a better choice than stainless steel, a poor conductor which may scorch and may not withstand very high temperatures. Nonstick woks can be generally useful and less oil or fat is necessary than with a traditional wok. However, they cannot be seasoned like a carbon steel wok and they must not be overheated. Electric woks cannot be used for authentic stir-frying as they do not heat to a high enough temperature and are too shallow.

The Cantonese wok has a short handle on either side and is used especially for steaming and deep-frying. The more round-bottomed Pau wok has one long handle, usually wooden, which does not get hot, so you can hold the wok with one hand, and stir with the other.

SEASONING THE WOK

Authentic carbon steel Chinese woks must be scrubbed to remove the protective coating of machine oil applied during manufacturing and seasoned before use. To remove the sometimes thick, sticky oil, scrub the wok vigorously with kitchen detergent and hot water. This is the only time you should scrub the wok, unless it rusts during storage. Dry the wok and place it over low heat for a few minutes, to dry thoroughly. To season, add 2 tablespoons vegetable oil and, using a double thickness of folded, paper towels, rub a thin film of oil all over the inside of the wok. Heat the wok for a few more minutes and wipe again. The paper will probably be black from machine oil residue. Repeat until the paper stays clean. The wok is now ready for use.

CLEANING THE WOK

Food rarely sticks to a seasoned wok, so an ordinary wash in hot water with no detergent should suffice. If any food has stuck, use a bamboo wok brush, or ordinary plastic kitchen scrubber. Dry the wok thoroughly and dry it over a low heat to prevent rust during storage. As a precaution, rub the inside surface of the dry wok with 1 teaspoon of oil. If the wok rusts, repeat the seasoning.

CUTTING AND COOKING TECHNIQUES

Cutting and slicing Chinese style is an art. The size and shape of ingredients determines cooking time, and there is little time for foods to absorb flavors and seasonings. Therefore, cut vegetables thinly, with as many cut surfaces as possible. Cut meats, fish and poultry generally across the grain, for maximum tenderness.

Slicing: Hold food firmly against a cutting board with one hand and, with a knife, slice food straight down into thin strips. Hold a cleaver with your index finger extended over the top edge and your thumb on the near side, to guide the cutting edge. Hold the food with the other hand, tucking your fingers under, so the blade rests against your knuckles for safety. For matchstick-thin strips, square off the sides of the prepared vegetable, cut crossways into 2-inch lengths. Stack a few slices and cut even lengthwise strips.

Shredding: Foods such as cabbage or spinach are easily shredded by piling up a few leaves and cutting lengthwise into thin, fine shreds. Roll large leaves, jellyroll style, before cutting, to reduce width. Meat and poultry breasts or cutlets are easier to shred if frozen for about 20 minutes first.

Horizontal Slicing: To cut thick foods into two or more thin pieces to be sliced or shredded, hold the cleaver or knife parallel to the cutting board. Place one hand flat on the food surface and press down while slicing horizontally into the food. Repeat if necessary.

Diagonal Slicing: Most long vegetables such as green onions, asparagus or zucchini look more attractive and more surface area is exposed for quicker cooking, if sliced on the diagonal. Angle the cleaver or knife and cut.

Roll Cutting: This is like diagonal cutting, but is suitable for larger or tougher, long vegetables, such as celery or large carrots. Make a diagonal slice at one end. Turn the vegetable 180 degrees and make another diagonal slice. Continue until the whole vegetable is cut into triangular pieces about 1-inch long.

Dicing: Cut food into slices, then into lengthwise sticks. Stack the sticks and cut crosswise into even-sized cubes.

Chopping: First cut the food into long strips, stack them and, holding them with one hand, fingers tucked under, cut crosswise with a knife or cleaver. Use a rocking motion, keeping the tip of the knife or cleaver against the cutting board and using the knuckles as a guide.

Stir-Frying: Probably the single most important technique in stir-frying, is preheating the wok. This prevents food sticking and absorbing excess oil. Place the wok over medium heat and wait a few minutes until the wok is very hot, then add the oil and swirl to quickly coat the bottom and sides of the wok with oil.

For recipes that begin by adding the flavoring ingredients, such as garlic, gingerroot and green onions to the oil, it should be only moderately hot or these delicate ingredients may burn or become bitter. If, however, the first ingredient added is a meat or hearty vegetable, make the oil very hot, just below smoking point. As other ingredients are added, stir-fry over high heat by stirring and tossing them with the metal spatula or spoon. Allow meat to rest a minute on one side before stirring, to cook and brown. Keep the food moving from the center, up and out onto the side. If a sauce to be thickened with cornstarch is added to the dish, remove the wok briefly from the heat and push the food away from the center so the sauce-thickening mixture goes directly to the bottom of the wok; stir vigorously and then continue tossing the ingredients in the boiling sauce to coat the food evenly.

──── STIR-FRY INGREDIENTS ────

Bamboo Shoots: Young, tender shoots from the bottom of bamboo shoots, these are crunchy but bland, absorbing stronger flavors. Sold fresh in ethnic markets or canned in supermarkets. Rinse canned ones before using.

Bean Curd: Bean curd, or tofu, is a nutritious, low-calorie food made from soy beans. Bland, with a soft-cheese texture, it absorbs other flavors. Stir-fry with care as even firm bean curd can disintegrate. Soft bean curd is mostly used in soups and sauces.

Black Beans: These small, fermented soy beans are very salty. Black bean sauce, in cans or bottles, is a quick, handy substitute.

Bok Choy: This mild vegetable with white stalks and dark green leaves is widely available in supermarkets.

Daikon: A long white, bland root vegetable with a crunchy texture: also called Japanese white radish.

Fish Sauce: Also called nuoc nam and nam pla, is made from salted, fermented anchovies and used in sauces, stir-fries and as a condiment. The lighter Vietnamese and Thai sauces are best. A little goes a long way. Keeps almost indefinitely.

Five-Spice Powder: A blend of cinnamon, cloves, star anise, fennel and Szechuan pepper, used in Chinese marinades and sauces. Sold in supermarkets and Asian markets.

Galangal: Known as Thai ginger or laos, this is used fresh, minced or sliced, in soups, sauces and stir-fries. Sold in Asian markets.

Gingerroot: This knobby roots' sweet spicy flavor is used in oriental soups, stir-fries and in fish dishes. Store in a dark place, but do not refrigerate.

Hoisin Sauce: This sweet-spicy, dark red-brown condiment is used in Chinese marinades, barbecue sauces and stir-fries. Made from soy flour, chiles, garlic, ginger and sugar. Excellent dipping sauce.

Jicama: A sweet, crunchy Mexican root vegetable similar to water chest-nuts. Add to salads and stir-fries. Peel before using.

Lemon Grass: A long, thin, lemony herb. Bruise the stems, then chop or slice. Grated lemon or lime peel can be used instead.

Noodles:
Bean Thread — Also called cellophane noodles, these transparent noodles are made from ground mung beans. Stir into soups or stir-fry with vegetables. Soak in warm water 5 minutes for general use, but use unsoaked if deep-frying.
Dried Chinese Spaghetti —This thin firm noodle cooks quickly: any thin spaghetti-type noodle can be substituted. Chinese egg noodles are also sold fresh in supermarkets and Asian markets.
Rice Sticks — Long, thin, dried noodles made from rice flour, rice sticks can be fried directly in hot oil and increase many times in volume. A good base for any Chinese-style dish.
Soba — This spaghetti-size noodle, made from buckwheat flour, is often used in Japanese soups. Ideal for cold noodle salads. Very quick cooking. Widely available in supermarkets and Asian markets.

Oriental Eggplant: These long, thin eggplant, are tastier than large egg-plants, do not need peeling and do not absorb as much oil. Sold in supermarkets and Asian markets.

Oyster Sauce: A thick, brown, bottled sauce with a nonfishy rich, subtle flavor, made from concentrated oysters and soy sauce. Often used in beef and vegetable stir-fry dishes.

Plum Sauce: A thick, sweet Cantonese condiment made from plums, apricots, garlic, chiles, sugar, vinegar and flavorings. Use as a dip or a base for barbecue sauces.

Radicchio: A small, slightly bitter, red-leaf chicory. Use shredded in stir-fries, risottos or salads. Sold in supermarkets or Italian markets.

Rice Vinegar: Use Japanese rice vinegar, mild and clear, for salad dressings, sauces and pickling. Chinese vinegar is not strong enough.

Rice Wine: Made from fermented rice and yeast, this mellow wine is widely drunk and used for cooking. Japanese rice wine, mirin, is sweetened sake. A dry sherry can be substituted for either type of rice wine.

Sesame Oil: Made from sesame seeds, this has a rich, golden-brown color and a nutty flavor and aroma. Has a low smoking point and can burn easily. As a seasoning, a teaspoon added to a stir-fry dish just before serving adds a delicious flavor.

Sesame Paste: Also known as tahini, this is made from ground sesame seeds. It is often combined with garlic, oil, lemon juice and seasonings and used as a Middle Eastern dipping sauce.

Sesame Seeds: Widely available, these add texture and flavor to stir-fry dishes. Dry-fry in the wok first to bring out flavor, then stir-fry and use as a garnish. Black sesame seeds can be interchanged with white ones.

Soy Sauces: This essential Chinese condiment, flavoring and dipping sauce is made from a fermented mixture of soybeans, flour and water. The more delicate light soy sauce is most com-mon. It is salty, but can be diluted with water. Dark soy sauce is thicker and sweeter, containing molasses or caramel. Japanese soy sauce, shoyu, is always naturally fermented.

Spring Roll Skins: These paper-thin, wheat-flour-dough skins are sometimes sold as lumpia skins. They are thinner and fry more crispy than thicker Cantonese egg roll skins.

Szechuan Peppercorns: These aro-matic, reddish-brown dried berries have a mildly spicy flavor. Toast in a dry wok or skillet before grinding.

Water Chestnuts: A starchy, bland, crunchy tuber. Use raw in salads or add to soups and stir-fries. Widely sold in cans, rinse in cold water or drop briefly into boiling water, then rinse to remove any metallic taste.

Won-ton Skins: These are smooth, wheat-flour dough wrappers, about 3-inches square, sold fresh and frozen in supermarkets and Asian markets.

Yellow Bean Paste/Sauce: This thick, spicy sauce is made from fermented yellow beans, flour and salt; use for flavoring fish, poultry and vegetables.

CREOLE-STYLE FISH

1/4 cup vegetable oil
1 teaspoon paprika
1 teaspoon dried leaf oregano
1/2 teaspoon each ground cumin and hot chili powder
1/4 teaspoon freshly ground black pepper
1/4 teaspoon hot pepper sauce (or to taste)
1-3/4 pounds firm white fish fillets, such as flounder,
    cut into 1-inch pieces
1 onion, chopped
3 garlic cloves, finely chopped
4 celery stalks, thinly sliced
1 green bell pepper, diced
1 red bell pepper, diced
1/2 pound fresh okra, sliced
1 (14-oz.) can chopped tomatoes
Oregano sprigs, to garnish

In a shallow dish, combine 2 tablespoons of the oil, paprika, oregano, cumin, chili powder, black pepper and hot pepper sauce. Add fish pieces and stir gently to coat. Allow to stand 15 minutes. Heat a wok over high heat until very hot. With a slotted spoon, drain fish pieces and, working in batches, if necessary, add to the wok. Stir-fry gently 2 minutes until pieces are firm. Remove to a bowl.

Heat remaining oil in the wok and add onion, garlic and celery. Stir-fry 1 to 2 minutes until onion begins to soften. Add bell peppers and okra and stir-fry 2 to 3 minutes. Add any remaining marinade and chopped tomatoes. Bring to a boil and simmer 4 to 5 minutes until slightly thickened, stirring frequently. Return fish pieces to wok and cook 1 minute to heat through. Serve with rice and garnish with oregano.

Makes 6 servings.

—SWEET & SOUR SWORDFISH—

3 tablespoons light soy sauce
2 tablespoons dry sherry or rice wine
3 teaspoons wine vinegar or cider vinegar
1 tablespoon sugar
2 teaspoons chili sauce or tomato ketchup
1 pound swordfish steaks, 1-inch thick
3 tablespoons vegetable oil
1 red bell pepper, cut into 1-inch pieces
1 green bell pepper, cut into 1-inch pieces
4 green onions, cut into 2-inch pieces
1 tablespoon cornstarch, dissolved in 1 tablespoon
   cold water
2/3 cup fish stock or chicken stock
Wild rice mixture, to serve

In a bowl, combine soy sauce, sherry or rice wine, vinegar, sugar and chili sauce or tomato ketchup. Cut swordfish into strips and stir into marinade to coat. Allow to stand 20 minutes. Heat a wok until very hot but not smoking; add 2 tablespoons of the oil and swirl to coat wok. With a slotted spoon, remove fish pieces from the marinade, draining off and reserving as much liquid as possible. Add fish to the wok and stir-fry 2 to 3 minutes, until fish is firm. With a slotted spoon, remove fish strips to a bowl.

Add remaining oil to the wok. Add bell peppers and stir-fry 2 to 3 minutes, until peppers begin to soften. Add green onions and stir-fry 1 more minute. Stir the cornstarch mixture and add the reserved marinade, then stir in the stock until well blended. Pour into the wok and bring to a boil, stirring frequently. Simmer 1 to 2 minutes until thickened. Return swordfish to the sauce and stir gently 1 minute to heat through. Serve with rice.

Makes 4 servings.

—INDONESIAN-STYLE HALIBUT—

4 halibut fillets, about 6 ounces each
Juice of 1 lime
2 teaspoons ground turmeric
1/2 cup vegetable oil
1 garlic clove, finely chopped
1/2-inch piece gingerroot, peeled and finely chopped
1 fresh red hot chile, seeded and chopped
1 onion, sliced lengthwise into thin wedges
2 teaspoons ground coriander
2/3 cup unsweetened coconut milk
1 teaspoon sugar
1/2 teaspoon salt
6 ounces snow peas
Cilantro sprigs, to garnish

Place fish fillets in a shallow dish. Sprinkle with lime juice and rub the turmeric into both sides of each fillet. Set aside. In a wok, heat half of the oil until hot, but not smoking; swirl to coat wok. Gently slide 2 of the fish fillets into the oil and fry 4 to 5 minutes, carefully turning once during cooking. Remove and drain on paper towels. Add remaining oil to wok and fry remaining fish fillets in the same way. Drain as before and keep fish fillets warm.

Pour off all but 1 tablespoon oil from wok. Add garlic, gingerroot and chile and stir-fry 1 minute. Add onion and coriander and stir-fry 2 minutes until onion begins to soften. Stir in coconut milk, sugar and salt and bring to a boil, adding a little more water if sauce is too thick. Stir in snow-peas and cook 1 minute, until they turn bright green. Spoon sauce over fish fillets and garnish with cilantro.

Makes 4 servings.

—— BLACKENED TUNA PIECES ——

1 teaspoon chili powder or to taste
1/2 teaspoon freshly ground pepper
1 teaspoon ground coriander
1/2 teaspoon ground cumin
1/2 teaspoon ground turmeric
1 teaspoon paprika
1/2 teaspoon dried leaf thyme
1/4 cup vegetable oil
3 tablespoons orange juice
3 tablespoons cider vinegar
1 tablespoon honey
4 tuna steaks, about 8 ounces each and 1 inch thick, cut
   into pieces
2 garlic cloves, finely chopped
4 green onions, thinly sliced
Brown rice pilaf, to serve

In a shallow dish, combine chili powder, pepper, coriander, cumin, turmeric, paprika and thyme. In another shallow dish, combine oil, orange juice, vinegar and honey. Toss tuna pieces in oil mixture to coat all sides, then dip each tuna piece into the spice mixture to coat each side evenly.

Heat dry wok over high heat until very hot. Add tuna pieces and stir-fry 3 to 5 minutes or until firm. Remove to warm plates. Add oil mixture to wok and stir to deglaze any spice mixture. Add garlic and green onions and stir-fry 1 to 2 minutes. Spoon sauce over tuna and serve with a brown rice pilaf.

Makes 4 servings.

—TUNA, TOMATO & PENNE—

2 tablespoons olive oil
1 onion, chopped
2 garlic cloves, finely chopped
1 (28-oz.) can peeled tomatoes
1 tablespoon tomato paste
1 tablespoon chopped fresh oregano or 1 teaspoon dried
   leaf oregano
1/3 cup sun-dried tomatoes in oil, drained and chopped
Salt and freshly ground pepper
12 ounces penne or rigatoni
1/3 cup ripe olives, coarsely chopped
2 tablespoons capers, drained
1 (7-oz.) can light tuna, drained
2 tablespoons chopped fresh parsley
Parmesan cheese, to garnish

Heat a wok until hot. Add the oil and swirl to coat wok. Add onion and garlic and stir-fry 1 to 2 minutes or until beginning to soften. Add the tomatoes, stirring to break up the large pieces. Stir in the tomato paste, oregano and sun-dried tomatoes. Bring to a boil and simmer 10 to 12 minutes or until sauce is slightly thickened. Season with salt and pepper. Meanwhile, in a large saucepan of boiling water, cook penne according to package directions.

Stir olives, capers and tuna into sauce. Drain pasta and add to tomato sauce, stirring gently to mix well. Stir in chopped parsley and serve immediately from the wok, or spoon into 4 pasta bowls. Using a vegetable peeler, shave flakes of Parmesan cheese over each serving. Or, grate Parmesan cheese over each serving.

Makes 4 servings.

— TUNA WITH SPICY SALSA —

2 tablespoons sesame oil
1 tablespoon light soy sauce
1 garlic clove, finely chopped
1-1/2 pounds tuna steaks, 1 inch thick, cut into chunks
2 tablespoons vegetable oil
8 ounces daikon, diced
1 small cucumber, peeled, seeded and diced
1 red bell pepper, diced
1 red onion, finely chopped
1 fresh hot red chile, seeded and finely chopped
2 tablespoons lime juice
1 teaspoon sugar
1 tablespoon sesame seeds, toasted
Lime wedges and cilantro sprigs, to garnish
Oriental noodles, to serve

In a shallow dish, combine 1 tablespoon of the sesame oil, soy sauce and garlic. Add tuna chunks and toss gently to coat. Allow to stand 15 minutes. Heat a wok until very hot; add 1 tablespoon of the vegetable oil and swirl to coat. Add daikon, cucumber, bell pepper, onion and chile and stir-fry 2 to 3 minutes or until vegetables begin to soften and turn a bright color. Stir in lime juice, sugar and remaining sesame oil and cook 30 seconds or until sugar dissolves. Remove to a bowl.

Add remaining vegetable oil to wok and, working in batches, if necessary, add fish chunks and stir-fry gently 2 to 3 minutes or until firm. Arrange fish on 4 dinner plates and sprinkle with the sesame seeds. Spoon some of the warm relish onto each plate and garnish with lime wedges and cilantro sprigs. Serve with noodles.

Makes 4 servings.

── SNAPPER WITH CAPELLINI ──

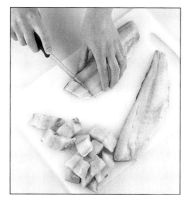

1 tablespoon olive oil
1/4 cup unsalted butter
1 pound red snapper or sea bass fillets, cut into 1-inch
   strips
Salt and freshly ground pepper
8 ounces mushrooms, quartered
2 garlic cloves, finely chopped
2/3 cup dry white wine
2 tomatoes, peeled, seeded and chopped
Juice of 1 lemon
1 tablespoon tomato paste
4 green onions, thinly sliced
2 tablespoons thinly shredded fresh basil
1 pound capellini or thin spaghetti
Basil sprigs, to garnish

Heat a wok until hot. Add oil and swirl to coat wok. Add half the butter and swirl to mix with oil. Add snapper and gently stir-fry 1 to 2 minutes or until just firm. Season with salt and pepper and, with a slotted spoon, remove to a bowl. Stir mushrooms into remaining oil and butter in the wok, then add garlic and stir-fry 1 minute. Add wine and stir to deglaze any bits stuck to wok. Bring to a boil and simmer 1 minute.

Stir in chopped tomatoes, lemon juice, tomato paste, green onions and basil. Stir in remaining butter in small pieces to thicken and smooth sauce. Return fish to sauce and cook gently 1 minute or until heated through. Meanwhile, in a large saucepan of boiling water, cook capellini or spaghetti according to package directions. Drain and divide among 4 plates. Top with fish strips and sauce and garnish with basil sprigs.

Makes 4 servings.

FIVE-SPICE SALMON

1 teaspoon sesame oil
3 tablespoons soy sauce
3 tablespoons dry sherry or rice wine
1 tablespoon honey
1 tablespoon lime juice or lemon juice
1 teaspoon five-spice powder
1-1/2 pounds salmon fillet, skinned and cut into 1-inch
  strips
2 egg whites
1 tablespoon cornstarch
1-1/4 cups vegetable oil
6 green onions, sliced into 2-inch pieces
1/2 cup light fish stock, chicken stock or water
Dash hot pepper sauce (optional)
Lime wedges, to garnish
Cooked rice, to serve

In a shallow baking dish, combine sesame oil, soy sauce, sherry, honey, lime juice and five-spice powder. Add salmon strips and toss gently to coat. Allow to stand 30 minutes. With a slotted spoon, remove the salmon strips from marinade and pat dry with paper towel. Reserve marinade. In a small dish, beat egg whites and cornstarch until soft peaks form. Add salmon strips and toss gently to coat completely.

Heat vegetable oil in the wok until hot. Add the salmon in batches. Fry 2 to 3 minutes until golden, turning once. Remove and drain on paper towels. Pour oil from wok into heatproof bowl and wipe wok clean. Pour marinade into wok and add green onions, stock and pepper sauce, if using. Bring to a boil and simmer 1 to 2 minutes. Add fish and turn gently to coat. Cook 1 minute until hot. Garnish with lime and serve with rice.

Makes 4 servings.

STEAMED SEA BASS

1 (2-1/4-lb.) sea bass, ready to cook with head and tail
    left on
1 tablespoon rice wine or dry sherry
1 teaspoon sea salt
1 tablespoon peanut oil
2 tablespoons fermented black beans, rinsed, drained
    and coarsely chopped
1 garlic clove, finely chopped
1/2-inch piece gingerroot, peeled and finely chopped
3 green onions, thinly sliced
2 tablespoons soy sauce
1/2 cup fish stock or chicken stock
6 teaspoons mild Chinese chili sauce
1 teaspoon sesame oil
Cilantro or green onions, to garnish

With a sharp knife, make 3 or 4 diagonal slashes 1/2 inch deep on both sides of fish. Sprinkle inside and out with wine and salt. Place in an oval baking dish which will fit in a wok. Allow to stand 20 minutes. Place a wire rack or 2 inverted ramekins in a wok. Fill wok with 1 inch of water and bring to a boil. Place dish with the fish on the rack or ramekins and cover tightly. Cook 8 to 12 minutes or until fish begins to flake. Remove fish from wok and keep warm. Remove rack or ramekins and pour off water. Wipe wok dry and reheat.

Add peanut oil and swirl to coat wok. Add the black beans, garlic and gingerroot and stir-fry 1 minute. Stir in the green onions, soy sauce and stock and bring to a boil; cook 1 minute. Stir in the chili sauce and sesame oil and remove from the heat. Pour sauce over fish and serve immediately, garnished with cilantro.

Makes 4 servings.

SINGAPORE CRAB

1 tablespoon vegetable oil
1 tablespoon sesame oil
4 garlic cloves, finely chopped
1-inch piece gingerroot, peeled and chopped
2 tablespoons wine vinegar
2/3 cup light fish stock or chicken stock
1/3 cup ketchup
1 tablespoon each hot chili sauce and soy sauce
1 tablespoon brown sugar
2-1/2 teaspoons cornstarch dissolved in 3 tablespoons
  water
4 green onions, thinly sliced
1 large cooked crab, cleaned and in the shell, chopped
  into serving pieces, with legs and claws cracked open,
  or 4 large crab claws, cracked open
Cucumber strips and cilantro leaves, to garnish

Heat a wok until very hot. Add the oils and swirl to coat wok. Add garlic and gingerroot and stir-fry 1 minute or until softened, but do not brown. Stir in vinegar, stock, ketchup, chili sauce, soy sauce and sugar and bring to a boil.

Stir the cornstarch mixture, and stir into wok with green onions and crab. Simmer crab in the sauce 2 to 4 minutes or until sauce thickens and crab is heated through. Garnish with cucumber and cilantro leaves. Serve with rice.

Makes 4 servings.

CRAB WON TONS

1/3 cup light soy sauce
2 tablespoons wine vinegar
2 tablespoons sesame oil
1 tablespoon water
1/2 teaspoon crushed dried chiles
2 teaspoons honey or sugar
6 to 8 canned whole water chestnuts, rinsed and
    minced
2 green onions, finely chopped
1 teaspoon finely chopped gingerroot
8 ounces white crabmeat, drained and picked over
1/2 teaspoon red pepper sauce
1 tablespoon finely chopped fresh cilantro or dill
1 egg yolk
30 won-ton skins
Vegetable oil for deep frying

In a small bowl, mix together 1/4 cup of the soy sauce, vinegar, 1 tablespoon of the sesame oil, water, crushed chiles and honey or sugar. Set aside. In a wok, heat remaining oils, add the water chestnuts, green onions and gingerroot and stir-fry 1 to 2 minutes. Cool slightly, then mix with crabmeat, remaining soy sauce, red pepper sauce, cilantro and egg yolk. Place a teaspoon of mixture in the center of each won-ton skin. Dampen edges with a little water and fold up one corner to opposite corner to form a triangle.

Fold over the bottom 2 corners to meet and press together to resemble a tortellini. Be sure the filling is well-sealed. In the wok, heat 3 inches of vegetable oil to 375F (190C) and deep-fry the won tons in batches 3 minutes or until golden on all sides, turning once during cooking. Remove with a Chinese strainer or slotted spoon to paper towels to drain. Serve with the dipping sauce.

Makes 30 won tons.

———— HOT SHRIMP SALAD ————

Mixed salad leaves
2 mangoes, sliced
2 tablespoons olive oil
5 ounces sugar snap peas
4 to 6 green onions, thinly sliced into 1-inch pieces
1 tablespoon butter
1 pound large shrimp, peeled and deveined
1 tablespoon anise-flavored liqueur
1/4 cup whipping cream
Pinch freshly grated nutmeg
Salt and freshly ground pepper
2 tablespoons chopped fresh dill
Dill sprigs, to garnish

Arrange the salad leaves on one side of 4 large plates and fan out the mango slices on the other side; set aside. Heat the oil in a wok and swirl to coat wok. Add sugar snap peas and green onions and stir-fry 1 to 2 minutes or until peas turn bright green and onions begin to soften. With a strainer or slotted spoon, remove to a bowl.

Add butter to oil in the wok and stir in shrimp. Stir-fry 1 to 2 minutes until heated through; do not overcook. Remove to the bowl. Pour in anise liqueur and stir to deglaze the wok. Cook 1 minute, then stir in cream and bring to a boil. Season with nutmeg, salt and pepper. Stir in dill, shrimp, peas and green onions, tossing to coat. Immediately, spoon mixture onto salad leaves and garnish with dill sprigs.

Makes 4 servings.

MONKFISH STIR-FRY

6-inch stalk fresh lemon grass, trimmed
1 teaspoon tomato paste
1 tablespoon vegetable oil
1 tablespoon sesame oil
1 pound monkfish, skinned and cut into chunks or
   1 pound cooked lobster meat
3 garlic cloves, finely chopped
1-inch piece gingerroot, peeled and chopped
1 white onion, cut lengthwise into thin wedges
1 fresh hot red chile, seeded and finely chopped
2 tomatoes, peeled, seeded and chopped
1 teaspoon sugar
2 large green onions, sliced into 1-inch pieces
2 tablespoons chopped cilantro
1 tablespoon lime juice
Lime wedges and cilantro, to garnish

Crush lemon grass and cut into 1-inch pieces. Place in a saucepan with 3/4 cup water and bring to a boil. Simmer 3 minutes. Add tomato paste and stir until dissolved. Set aside. Heat the oils in a wok until very hot. Add fish and stir-fry 3 or 4 minutes or until firm. Transfer fish to a bowl. If using lobster, stir-fry 1 to 2 minutes, then transfer to a bowl. Add garlic and gingerroot to wok and stir-fry 10 seconds. Add white onion and chile and stir-fry 1 to 2 minutes or until onion begins to soften. Add tomatoes, sugar and lemon grass mixture.

Add green onions, chopped cilantro and lime juice; cook 1 minute or until green onions turn bright green. Return fish or lobster to wok and cook 1 minute or until heated through. Serve immediately, garnished with lime and cilantro. Accompany with noodles.

Makes 2 servings.

Note: Monkfish is often called 'poor man's lobster' due to its sweet flavor and firm, lobsterlike texture.

- LOBSTER IN MUSTARD CREAM -

1 pound new potatoes, cut in half, if large
1 tablespoon butter
1 onion, finely chopped
1 garlic clove, finely chopped
1/2 pound mushrooms
1/2 cup dry white wine
1 cup whipping cream
Pinch freshly grated nutmeg
Salt and freshly ground pepper
4 green onions, thinly sliced
1 to 2 tablespoons Dijon-style mustard
1 pound cooked lobster meat
1/2 pound peeled cooked shrimp, thawed and patted
   dry, if frozen
2 tablespoons shredded fresh basil
Basil leaves, to garnish

In a saucepan of boiling water, cook new potatoes 12 to 15 minutes or until tender when pierced with a sharp knife. Heat a wok until hot. Add butter and swirl to melt and coat wok. Add onion and garlic and stir-fry 1 minute. Add mushrooms and stir-fry 1 to 2 minutes. Add white wine and bring to a boil. Simmer 2 to 3 minutes until reduced by half. Stir in the cream and bring back to a boil. Simmer 5 to 6 minutes until reduced and thickened. Season with nutmeg, salt and pepper and stir in green onions.

Stir in 1 tablespoon mustard, lobster and shrimp and cook 1 to 2 minutes. Add chopped basil and new potatoes. Taste and stir in remaining mustard for a stronger flavor. Spoon onto dinner plates and garnish with fresh basil leaves.

Makes 4 servings.

Variation: Cooked shrimp can be substituted for the lobster meat. Or substitute 1-1/2 pounds cooked monkfish pieces for the lobster and shrimp.

——CHILE CUCUMBER SHRIMP——

1 pound cooked unpeeled shrimp
1 tablespoon vegetable oil
1 tablespoon sesame oil
1-inch piece gingerroot, peeled and finely chopped
2 to 3 garlic cloves, finely minced
2 to 3 fresh hot red chiles, seeded and chopped
1/2 cucumber, peeled, seeded and diced
2 to 3 green onions, thinly sliced
2 tablespoons ketchup
1 tablespoon white-wine vinegar
1/2 teaspoon sugar

Using kitchen scissors or a small sharp knife, cut along backs of shrimp shells to expose the black vein. Keeping shells intact, rinse out the vein under cold water. Pat shrimp dry with a paper towel. Heat a wok until hot. Add oils, swirling to coat wok. Add gingerroot, garlic and chiles and stir-fry 1 minute until very fragrant but not browned. Increase heat and add the shrimp. Stir-fry 1 to 2 minutes until shrimp are hot.

Stir in the cucumber and green onions. Add ketchup, vinegar and sugar and stir-fry 1 minute, until shrimp are lightly coated with sauce and cucumbers look translucent. Serve immediately.

Makes 2 servings.

—JASMINE-SCENTED SHRIMP—

3 tablespoons rice wine, sake or dry sherry
1 tablespoon light soy sauce
1-inch piece gingerroot, peeled and finely chopped
1 teaspoon sesame oil
1/4 teaspoon salt
1-1/2 pounds raw medium-size shrimp, shelled and
    deveined
2 tablespoons jasmine or other aromatic tea leaves,
    such as Earl Grey
1/2 cup light fish or chicken stock
2 teaspoons cornstarch dissolved in 1 tablespoon water
1/2 teaspoon sugar
1 tablespoon vegetable oil
4 green onions, thinly sliced
Mint sprigs or jasmine flowers, to garnish

In a medium-size bowl, combine rice wine, sake or dry sherry, soy sauce, gingerroot, sesame oil and salt. Add shrimp and toss to coat well. Let stand 30 minutes, stirring once or twice. In a small bowl, stir the tea leaves into 1/2 cup boiling water and steep 1 minute. Strain tea through a fine tea strainer into another bowl and discard the tea leaves. Add stock to the tea and stir in the cornstarch mixture and sugar.

Heat wok until hot, add vegetable oil and swirl to coat wok. With a Chinese strainer or slotted spoon, remove shrimp from marinade. Working in batches, add shrimp to wok and stir-fry 1 to 2 minutes until pink and firm; remove to a bowl. Stir in green onions and reserved marinade and cook 1 minute. Stir tea mixture and add to wok, cook, stirring, until thickened. Return shrimp to wok and toss lightly to coat. Garnish with mint or jasmine and serve with rice.

Makes 4 servings.

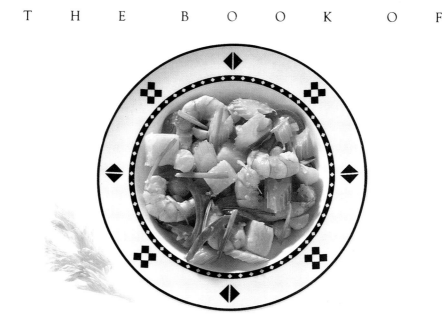

PACIFIC SHRIMP

2 tablespoons peanut oil
1 pound raw medium-size shrimp, shelled and deveined
2 garlic cloves, finely chopped
1-inch piece gingerroot, peeled and finely chopped
2 celery stalks, sliced
1 red bell pepper, sliced
4 green onions, cut into thin strips
1 (8-oz.) can unsweetened pineapple chunks, drained,
    juice reserved
2 teaspoons cornstarch
2 teaspoons soy sauce
1 tablespoon lemon juice
Dash of hot pepper sauce
1 cup macadamia nuts, rinsed lightly if salted

Heat a wok until hot. Add 1 tablespoon of the oil and swirl to coat wok. Add shrimp and stir-fry 2 minutes or until shrimp turn pink and feel firm to the touch. Remove to a bowl. Add remaining oil to wok. Add garlic and gingerroot and stir-fry 30 seconds. Stir in celery, bell pepper and green onions and stir-fry 3 or 4 minutes or until vegetables are tender but still crisp. Stir in the pineapple chunks.

Dissolve cornstarch in the reserved pineapple juice. Stir in soy sauce, lemon juice and hot pepper sauce. Stir into the vegetable mixture and bring to a simmer. Add reserved shrimp and macadamia nuts and stir-fry until sauce thickens and shrimp are heated through.

Makes 4 servings.

— SHRIMP WITH RADICCHIO —

2 tablespoons olive oil
4 garlic cloves, finely chopped
2 shallots, finely chopped
2 prosciutto slices, diced
1-1/2 pounds raw medium-size shrimp, shelled and
  deveined
1/2 cup grappa or brandy
1/2 pound radicchio, thinly shredded
1 cup whipping cream
Salt and freshly ground pepper
3 or 4 tablespoons chopped fresh parsley
1 pound linguine

Heat a wok until hot. Add oil; swirl to coat wok. Add garlic, shallots and prosciutto.

Stir-fry 2 minutes or until prosciutto is crisp. Add shrimp and stir-fry 2 minutes or until shrimp turn pink and feel firm to the touch. With a Chinese strainer or slotted spoon, remove shrimp mixture to a bowl. Add grappa and bring to a boil, stirring frequently. Stir in radicchio, cream, salt and pepper and bring to a simmer; cook 1 minute or until sauce thickens slightly. Return shrimp to wok and stir to coat. Stir in half of the parsley.

In a large saucepan of boiling water, cook linguine according to package directions. Drain and divide among 4 large bowls. Top with equal amounts of shrimp and sauce and sprinkle with remaining parsley.

Makes 4 servings.

Variation: Cooked shrimp can be substituted for raw shrimp. Add to thickened sauce and heat until hot before adding parsley.

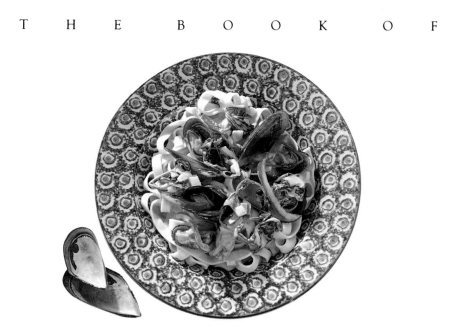

—MUSSELS WITH WATERCRESS—

36 to 40 large mussels
2 tablespoons olive oil
1 onion, finely chopped
2 garlic cloves, finely chopped
1 cup light fish stock or chicken stock
1 small bell red pepper, thinly sliced
2/3 cup whipping cream
2 bunches watercress or arugula, chopped
Salt and freshly ground black pepper
1 pound tagliatelle

With a stiff brush, scrub mussels. Discard any that are not tightly closed. Using a small knife, remove beards and barnacles.

Heat a wok until hot. Add olive oil and swirl to coat wok. Add the onion and garlic and stir-fry 2 minutes or until onion begins to soften. Stir in stock and mussels. Bring to a boil, cover and simmer 3 minutes or until mussels open. Using a Chinese strainer, scoop out the mussels into a large bowl; discard any unopened mussels. If desired, remove and discard half of the mussel shells.

Add the bell pepper and boil the cooking liquid until reduced to about 1 cup. Add cream and simmer 3 minutes or until slightly thickened. Stir in watercress and season with salt and black pepper. Return the mussels to the sauce; cook, stirring, to heat through. In a large saucepan of boiling water, cook the tagliatelle according to package directions. Drain and divide among 4 soup plates. Top with equal amounts of mussels and sauce.

Makes 4 servings.

OYSTER WOK STEW

Olive oil for deep-frying
1 small loaf French bread, cut into 1/2-inch cubes
Freshly ground pepper
Parmesan cheese for sprinkling
1 tablespoon butter
1 small onion, finely chopped
1 garlic clove, finely minced
2 tablespoons all-purpose flour
1 (14-oz.) can chopped tomatoes, drained
1/2 teaspoon chili powder or to taste
1/2 teaspoon paprika
24 to 30 shucked oysters, liquid reserved
2 cups whipping cream
1 cup milk
2 tablespoons chopped fresh parsley

Heat 2 inches of oil in a wok until very hot, but not smoking. Add bread cubes and, working in batches, deep-fry 1 minute or until golden. Drain on paper towels, then sprinkle with pepper and Parmesan cheese, tossing to coat. Pour off all but 1 tablespoon oil and return wok to heat. Add butter, onion and garlic and stir-fry 2 minutes or until onion begins to soften. Add flour and cook 1 minute. Add tomatoes, chili powder and paprika and cook 3 minutes or until thickened, stirring frequently.

Pour reserved oyster liquid through a cheesecloth-lined strainer into tomato mixture. Stir in whipping cream and milk and slowly bring to a simmer. Cook 5 minutes or until sauce thickens and reduces slightly. Add oysters to liquid and simmer 2 minutes or until edges of the oysters begin to curl. Stir in chopped parsley and pour into soup plates. If desired, sprinkle with extra Parmesan and pass croutons separately.

Makes 4 to 6 servings.

MALAY CURRIED CLAMS

24 steamer clams
1 tablespoon vegetable oil
1 tablespoon sesame oil
2 garlic cloves, finely chopped
1-inch piece gingerroot, peeled and finely chopped
1 tablespoon fermented black beans, rinsed and
    chopped
1 tablespoon curry paste or 2 tablespoons curry powder
1 cup light fish stock or chicken stock
1/4 cup ketchup
2 tablespoons oyster sauce
1 tablespoon soy sauce
1 teaspoon Chinese chili sauce
2 teaspoons cornstarch dissolved in 3 tablespoons
    water
4 green onions, thinly sliced

With a stiff brush, scrub clams well. Cover
with cold water and soak about 1 hour. With
a Chinese strainer, carefully remove clams
from soaking liquid to a colander. (This
leaves any sand or grit on the bottom.)
Discard any clams that are not tightly closed.
Heat oils in a wok, swirling to mix oils and
coat wok. Add garlic, gingerroot and black
beans and stir-fry 30 seconds or until fragrant.
Stir in curry paste and cook 1 minute, stirring
constantly.

Stir in clams, stock, ketchup, oyster sauce,
soy sauce and chili sauce. Bring to a boil,
reduce heat, cover and simmer about 5
minutes or until clams open. Stir cornstarch
mixture and stir into clams with green
onions. Stir until sauce thickens and green
onions turn a bright color. Discard any
unopened clams. Serve immediately with
steamed rice or noodles.

Makes 2 servings..

SWEET & SOUR SCALLOPS

6-inch stalk fresh lemon grass, trimmed
2 tablespoons peanut oil
2 garlic cloves, finely chopped
1-inch piece gingerroot, peeled and finely chopped
1 fresh hot red chile, seeded and chopped
1 pound scallops, with roe (optional), cut in half
   crosswise
1 green bell pepper, diced
1 red bell pepper, diced
4 to 6 green onions, thinly sliced
1/3 cup seasoned rice vinegar
2 to 3 tablespoons nam pla (Thai fish sauce)
1 teaspoon sugar
1 tomato, peeled, seeded and chopped
3 tablespoons chopped fresh cilantro, plus sprigs, to
   garnish

Crush lemon grass stalk and cut into 1/2-inch pieces. Heat a wok until hot, add the oil and swirl to coat wok. Add lemon grass, garlic, gingerroot and chile and stir-fry 30 seconds. Add scallops and stir-fry 3 minutes or until they are opaque and slightly firm to the touch. With a Chinese strainer or slotted spoon, remove to a bowl.

Add bell peppers and green onions to wok and stir-fry 2 or 3 minutes or until vegetables begin to soften. Add vinegar, nam pla, sugar, tomato and chopped cilantro. Return scallops to wok and toss 30 to 50 seconds to coat with the sauce and heat through. Garnish with cilantro sprigs and serve with mixed white and wild rice.

Makes 4 servings.

— SCALLOPS WITH CASHEWS —

1/4 cup dry sherry or rice wine
3 tablespoons ketchup
1 tablespoon oyster sauce
1 tablespoon white-wine vinegar
1 tablespoon sesame oil
1 teaspoon Chinese chili sauce (or to taste)
1 tablespoon each grated orange zest and orange juice
1 teaspoon cornstarch
1 tablespoon vegetable oil
1/2 pound bay scallops, with roe (optional)
2 garlic cloves, finely chopped
4 green onions, thinly sliced
6 ounces asparagus, cut into 1-inch pieces
5 ounces cashew nuts, lightly rinsed

In a medium-size bowl, combine sherry, ketchup, oyster sauce, vinegar, sesame oil, chili sauce, orange zest, orange juice and cornstarch. Heat a wok until hot, add oil and swirl to coat wok. Add scallops and stir-fry 1 or 2 minutes or until they begin to turn opaque. Remove to a bowl.

Add garlic, green onions and asparagus to wok and stir-fry 2 or 3 minutes or until asparagus is bright green and tender but still crisp. Stir sauce ingredients and pour into wok. Bring to a simmer. Return scallops to wok and add the cashews. Stir-fry 1 minute or until scallops are heated through, tossing to coat all ingredients. Serve with rice garnished with strips of orange peel.

Makes 4 servings.

THAI CURRIED SEAFOOD

2 tablespoons vegetable oil
1 pound scallops, cut in half lengthwise
1 onion, chopped
2-inch piece gingerroot, peeled and finely chopped
4 garlic cloves, finely chopped
1 tablespoon curry paste or 2 tablespoons curry powder
1-1/2 teaspoons each ground coriander and cumin
6-inch piece stalk lemon grass, crushed
1 (8-oz.) can chopped tomatoes
1/2 cup chicken stock
2 cups unsweetened coconut milk
12 mussels, scrubbed and debearded
1 pound cooked, peeled shrimp, deveined
12 crab legs, meat removed, cut into 1/2-inch pieces
Chopped cilantro and shaved coconut, to garnish

Heat a wok until hot and add 1 tablespoon of the oil, swirl to coat wok. Add scallops and stir-fry 2 or 3 minutes or until opaque and firm. Remove to a bowl. Add remaining oil to wok and add onion, gingerroot and garlic. Stir-fry 1 or 2 minutes or until onion begins to soften. Add curry paste, coriander, cumin and lemon grass. Stir-fry 1 or 2 minutes. Add tomatoes and stock. Bring to a boil, stirring frequently. Simmer 5 minutes or until slightly reduced and thickened. Add the coconut milk and simmer 2 or 3 minutes.

Stir mussels into sauce and cook, covered, 1 or 2 minutes or until mussels begin to open. Stir in shrimp, crab sticks and reserved scallops. Cook, covered, 1 or 2 minutes more or until all mussels open and seafood is heated through. Remove the lemon grass stalk and discard any mussels that have not opened. Garnish with chopped cilantro and shaved coconut.

Makes 6 to 8 servings.

SEAFOOD JAMBALAYA

2 tablespoons vegetable oil
1 pound raw medium-size shrimp, shelled and deveined
1/2 pound sea scallops
1/2 pound pork sausage meat
1 tablespoon all-purpose flour
1 large onion, chopped
3 garlic cloves, chopped
2 celery stalks, thinly sliced
1 each green and red bell pepper, diced
1 tablespoon Cajun seasoning mix or chili powder
1-1/2 cups long-grain rice
1 (14-oz.) can chopped tomatoes
2 cups chicken stock
Salt and freshly ground black pepper
1 pound cooked crayfish tails or meat from 2 crabs
Chopped fresh parsley, to garnish

Heat wok until hot, add oil and swirl to coat wok. Add shrimp and stir-fry 2 or 3 minutes or until shrimp turn pink and feel firm to touch. Remove to a bowl. Add scallops to wok and stir-fry 2 or 3 minutes or until opaque and firm. Remove scallops to bowl. Stir sausage meat into wok and stir-fry 4 or 5 minutes or until well browned. Stir flour into sausage meat until completely blended, then add onion, garlic, celery, bell peppers and Cajun seasoning mix. Stir-fry 4 or 5 minutes or until vegetables begin to soften, then stir in rice.

Add chopped tomatoes with their liquid and chicken stock; stir well and season with salt and black pepper. Bring to a simmer and cook, covered, 20 minutes or until rice is tender and liquid is absorbed. Stir in reserved shrimp, scallops and cooked crayfish tails or crab pieces and cook, covered, 5 minutes more or until seafood is heated through. Garnish with fresh parsley.

Makes 6 servings.

—— CHILE-CHICKEN SALAD ——

1-1/2 pounds skinless boneless chicken breasts
1-1/4 cups brown rice
3 tablespoons sesame oil
2 tablespoons peanut oil
1 cup cashew nuts or peanuts
5 ounces snow peas
2 tablespoons sunflower oil
1-inch fresh gingerroot, peeled and thinly sliced
2 garlic cloves, finely chopped
4 to 6 green onions, sliced
1 or 2 fresh green chiles, seeded and thinly sliced
3 tablespoons white-wine vinegar
1 tablespoon shredded fresh mint or cilantro
Mixed lettuce leaves
1 orange, peeled, segmented and any juice reserved
Chopped fresh herbs, to garnish

Cut chicken into thin strips. Cook rice according to package directions until tender. Drain and place in a large bowl; toss with sesame oil and set aside. Heat a wok until hot, add peanut oil and swirl to coat wok. Add the nuts and stir-fry 1 or 2 minutes or until they turn golden. Remove and add to rice. Add snow peas to oil in wok and stir-fry 1 or 2 minutes or until bright green. Add to the rice. Add chicken strips to wok in 2 batches, and stir-fry 2 or 3 minutes or until chicken turns white and feels firm to the touch. Add to the rice.

Add sunflower oil to wok and stir in ginger-root, garlic, green onions and chile. Stir-fry 1 minute or until onion begins to soften. Pour contents of wok over rice mixture. Return wok to heat and pour in vinegar, swirling to deglaze wok. Pour vinegar over rice mixture, add mint and toss to mix well. Line a shallow serving bowl with lettuce. Spoon rice mixture over lettuce, decorate with orange segments and pour over any reserved juice. Garnish with chopped herbs.

Makes 4 servings.

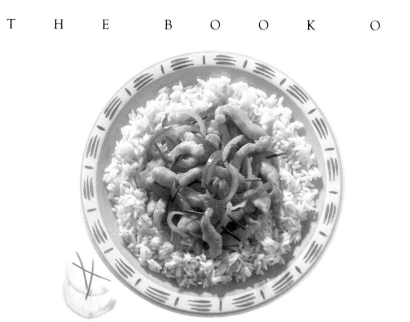

LEMON CHICKEN

2 egg whites
7 teaspoons cornstarch
1-1/4 pounds skinless boneless chicken breasts, cut
  into thin strips
1/2 cup vegetable oil
1 onion, thinly sliced
1 garlic clove, finely chopped
1 red bell pepper, thinly sliced
2/3 cup chicken stock
Grated peel and juice of 1 lemon
1 tablespoon sugar
1 tablespoon light soy sauce
1 tablespoon rice wine or dry sherry
Dash of hot pepper sauce
Fresh chives, to garnish
Rice, to serve

In a medium-size bowl, beat egg whites with 4 teaspoons cornstarch. Add the chicken strips and toss to coat well. Refrigerate 10 to 15 minutes. In a wok, heat the vegetable oil until very hot and swirl to coat wok. Using tongs or a fork, add the chicken strips, a few at a time. Stir-fry quickly to keep strips from sticking. Cook chicken strips 2 or 3 minutes until just golden. Remove to paper towel to drain and pour off all but 1 tablespoon oil. (Reserve oil for future frying or discard.)

Add onion, garlic and bell pepper to wok. Stir-fry 1 or 2 minutes or until onion begins to soften. Add chicken stock, lemon peel, lemon juice, sugar, soy sauce, wine and hot pepper sauce. Dissolve remaining cornstarch in 2 tablespoons water and stir into the sauce. Cook 30 seconds or until sauce thickens. Add chicken strips and toss to coat. Cook 1 minute or until chicken is heated through. Garnish with chives and serve with rice.

Makes 4 servings.

YELLOW BEAN CHICKEN

2 egg whites
4 teaspoons cornstarch
1-1/2 pounds skinless boneless chicken breasts or
    thighs, cut into 1-inch cubes
1/2 cup peanut oil
4 green onions, sliced
2 celery stalks, thinly sliced
1 green bell pepper, diced
1 teaspoon finely chopped gingerroot
1 teaspoon crushed dried chiles
1 teaspoon sugar
4 teaspoons yellow bean paste
4 teaspoons dry sherry or rice wine
1 cup cashew nuts, toasted
Lemon wedges, to serve

In a medium-size bowl, beat egg whites with the cornstarch. Add chicken cubes, tossing to coat well. Refrigerate 10 to 15 minutes. In a wok, heat peanut oil until very hot and swirl to coat wok. Using a slotted spoon, and work-ing in 2 batches, lift out chicken cubes and add to wok. Stir-fry quickly to keep cubes from sticking. Cook chicken cubes 2 or 3 minutes or until just golden. Remove to paper towels to drain and pour off all but 2 tablespoons oil. (Reserve oil for future frying or discard).

Add green onions, celery, bell pepper and gingerroot and stir-fry 2 or 3 minutes or until onion and bell pepper begin to soften. Stir in the crushed chiles, sugar, yellow bean paste, sherry and cashew nuts, tossing until sugar dissolves. Add chicken cubes and toss to coat; cook 30 seconds. Serve immediately with lemon wedges and accompanied with salad.

Makes 4 servings.

— ARABIAN CHICKEN IN PITA —

2-1/4 pounds skinless boneless chicken breasts, cut
   into thin slices
1/2 teaspoon salt
1/2 teaspoon freshly ground black pepper
1/2 teaspoon ground cardamom
1/2 teaspoon ground cinnamon
1/4 teaspoon ground cloves
1/4 teaspoon ground allspice
1/4 teaspoon red (cayenne) pepper or chili powder
2 tablespoons lemon juice
2 tablespoons olive oil
3 (8-inch) pita breads
6 lettuce leaves
1 onion, finely chopped
Bottled tahini sauce
Basil sprigs and onion rings, to garnish

Place chicken into a large shallow baking
dish. Combine salt and spices in a small bowl.
Combine chicken, spice mixture and lemon
juice until chicken is coated, then cover and
marinate in the refrigerator 4 to 6 hours or
overnight. Heat a wok until hot. Add olive
oil and swirl to coat wok. Add coated chicken
pieces, and working in 2 batches, stir-fry 2 or
3 minutes or until just golden and firm to the
touch. Remove chicken to paper towels to
drain.

Preheat broiler. Arrange pitas on a broiler
pan and heat under broiler 1 or 2 minutes,
turning once during cooking, or until pitas
are puffed and golden. Cut each pita crosswise in half to open, and place a lettuce leaf
in each half. Spoon equal amounts of chicken
strips into pitas, sprinkle with chopped onion
and drizzle with tahini sauce. Garnish with
basil sprigs and onion rings.

Makes 6 servings.

CHICKEN IN BALSAMIC VINEGAR

Mixed salad leaves
2 tablespoons olive oil
1 onion, finely chopped
2 garlic cloves, finely minced or crushed
1-1/2 pounds skinless boneless chicken breasts, cut
    into 1-inch strips
3 tablespoons balsamic vinegar
1 tablespoon Dijon-style mustard
Freshly ground pepper
2 tablespoons shredded fresh basil
Basil leaves, to garnish

Arrange salad leaves on 4 dinner plates and
set aside.

Heat a wok until hot. Add olive oil and swirl
to coat wok. Add onion and garlic and stir-fry
1 or 2 minutes or until onion begins to soften.
Add chicken strips, working in 2 batches,
and stir-fry 3 or 4 minutes or until golden and
chicken feels firm to the touch. Return all
chicken to wok.

Stir in vinegar and mustard and stir-fry 2 or 3
minutes or until chicken is cooked through
and coated with vinegar and mustard. Season
with pepper and sprinkle with shredded basil.
Spoon onto salad-lined plates and garnish
with basil leaves.

Makes 4 servings.

—— SATAY-STYLE CHICKEN ——

Lettuce leaves and 1 cucumber, cut into julienned
   strips
3 tablespoons peanut oil
1-inch piece gingerroot, peeled and finely chopped
1 garlic clove, finely chopped
1-1/4 pounds skinless boneless chicken thighs, cut into
   small pieces
1 teaspoon chili powder
2 tablespoons smooth peanut butter
2 tablespoons Chinese chili sauce
4 to 6 green onions, thinly sliced
1-1/4 cups unsweetened coconut milk
1 teaspoon sugar
1/2 teaspoon salt
Chopped peanuts and cilantro leaves, to garnish

Arrange lettuce leaves and cucumber on a
shallow serving dish and set aside. Heat a wok
until hot. Add oil and swirl to coat wok. Add
gingerroot and garlic and stir-fry 1 minute or
until fragrant; do not brown. Add chicken
and stir-fry 3 or 4 minutes or until just golden
and pieces feel slightly firm to the touch.

Stir in chili powder, peanut butter, chili
sauce and green onions. Slowly add coconut
milk, stirring until sauce is smooth. Add
sugar and salt and simmer 3 to 5 minutes or
until sauce is thickened. Spoon onto a
serving dish and sprinkle with chopped
peanuts and cilantro leaves.

Makes 4 servings.

BANG BANG CHICKEN

4 tablespoons peanut oil
3 carrots, cut into julienne strips
1 fresh hot red chile, seeded and chopped
1/2 pound bean sprouts, trimmed
1/2 cucumber, seeded and cut into julienne strips
1-3/4 pounds skinned and boned chicken breasts, cut
  into shreds
1-inch fresh gingerroot, cut in julienne strips
2 garlic cloves, finely chopped
4 green onions, thinly sliced
3 tablespoons cider vinegar or rice vinegar
2 tablespoons dry sherry or rice wine
1 tablespoon sugar
1 teaspoon Chinese chili sauce
2/3 cup chicken stock
3 tablespoons each light soy sauce and tahini

Heat wok until hot. Add 2 tablespoons of the peanut oil and swirl to coat wok. Add carrots and chile and stir-fry 2 or 3 minutes. Remove to a bowl. Stir-fry bean sprouts 1 minute and remove to bowl. Add cucumber to bowl. Heat remaining oil in wok and add chicken. Working in 2 batches, stir-fry 2 or 3 minutes or until the chicken is white and the juices run clear. Remove to another bowl. Increase heat, add gingerroot and garlic to wok and stir-fry 1 minute. Add green onions and stir-fry 1 minute. Add remaining ingredients and stir-fry until sauce is smooth and thick.

Pour half the sauce over carrot mixture and remaining sauce over chicken; toss each mixture well. Spoon chicken onto center of a serving dish, then spoon vegetables around chicken.

Makes 6 servings.

— MOROCCAN-STYLE CHICKEN —

3 pounds chicken, cut into 8 pieces
4 tablespoons olive oil
Grated peel and juice of 1 lemon
1 teaspoon each ground cinnamon, ground ginger and
    ground cumin
1/2 teaspoon salt
1/2 teaspoon red (cayenne) pepper or to taste
1 onion, chopped
3 or 4 garlic cloves, finely chopped
1 red bell pepper, diced
1 tomato, peeled, seeded and chopped
1 cup chicken stock or water
16 pitted prunes
1/4 cup honey
1 large lemon, thinly sliced
Toasted almonds and chopped fresh parsley, to garnish

In a large shallow baking dish, combine chicken pieces with 2 tablespoons of the olive oil, the lemon peel, lemon juice, cinnamon, ginger, cumin, salt and cayenne. Work the spice mixture into the chicken pieces, cover and marinate in the refrigerator 4 to 6 hours or overnight. Heat a wok until hot. Add 1 tablespoon oil and swirl to coat wok. Arrange marinated chicken pieces on bottom and side of wok in a single layer and stir-fry 6 to 8 minutes or until golden. Remove chicken pieces to a clean baking dish.

Add remaining oil, onion, garlic and bell pepper to wok. Stir-fry 2 or 3 minutes. Add tomato and stock and bring to a simmer, stirring. Return chicken and marinade to sauce. Simmer, covered, 20 minutes. Add prunes, honey and lemon slices. Simmer 20 minutes or until chicken is tender. Remove chicken to a serving dish, spoon sauce over chicken and sprinkle with almonds and parsley. Serve with couscous.

Makes 4 servings.

——— SPICY CHICKEN WINGS ———

1 tablespoon light soy sauce
1 tablespoon dry sherry or rice wine
2-1/2 pounds chicken wings, tips removed and wings
    cut into 2 pieces at joint
1 tablespoon peanut oil
1-inch piece gingerroot, peeled and finely chopped
2 garlic cloves, finely chopped
3 tablespoons fermented black beans, coarsely chopped
1/2 cup chicken stock
2 tablespoons soy sauce
1 teaspoon Chinese chili sauce
4 to 6 green onions, thinly sliced
6 ounces small green beans, cut into 2-inch pieces
2 tablespoons chopped peanuts and fresh cilantro
    leaves, to garnish

In a shallow baking dish, combine soy sauce, sherry and chicken wings. Toss well and marinate, covered, 1 hour. Heat a wok until hot. Add peanut oil and swirl to coat wok. Add gingerroot and garlic and stir-fry 1 minute. Add chicken wings and, working in 2 batches, stir-fry 3 to 5 minutes or until golden. Stir in black beans, stock, soy sauce and chili sauce. Return all chicken wings to wok.

Bring to a boil, reduce the heat and cook 4 to 6 minutes, stirring frequently. Stir in green onions and green beans and cook 2 or 3 minutes more or until chicken is tender and juices run clear. Sprinkle with peanuts and garnish with cilantro leaves.

Makes 4 to 6 servings.

—TANGERINE CHICKEN WINGS—

1 onion, thinly sliced
1-inch piece gingerroot, peeled and thinly sliced
1 teaspoon sea salt
4 tablespoons dry sherry or rice wine
4 tablespoons soy sauce
16 chicken wings, wing tips removed
1 large tangerine
1/3 cup vegetable oil
2 fresh hot red chiles, seeded and chopped
4 green onions, thinly sliced
2 teaspoons sugar
1 tablespoon white-wine vinegar
1 teaspoon sesame oil
Cilantro sprigs, to garnish

In a large shallow baking dish, combine onion, gingerroot, salt, 1 tablespoon of the sherry and 1 tablespoon of the soy sauce. Add chicken wings and toss to coat well. Let stand 30 minutes. Remove peel from tangerine and slice thinly. Squeeze 2 or 3 tablespoons tangerine juice and reserve. Heat oil in a wok until hot and swirl to coat wok. Remove chicken from the marinade, returning any onion or gingerroot sticking to it. Working in 2 batches, add chicken wings to wok. Fry 3 or 4 minutes or until golden, turning once. Drain on paper towels.

Pour off all but 1 tablespoon oil from wok. Add chiles, green onions and tangerine peel and stir-fry 30 to 40 seconds. Pour in reserved marinade with the onion and gingerroot slices. Add sugar, vinegar and remaining sherry, remaining soy sauce and the tangerine juice. Add the chicken wings and toss to coat well; cook 1 minute or until heated through. Drizzle with sesame oil and garnish with cilantro sprigs. Serve with noodles tossed in sesame oil.

Makes 4 servings.

—BOMBAY CHICKEN THIGHS—

2 tablespoons vegetable oil
1-inch piece gingerroot, peeled and finely chopped
2 garlic cloves, finely chopped
1 fresh hot red chile, seeded and chopped
1-1/2 pounds skinless boneless chicken thighs,
    cut into pieces
1 onion, coarsely chopped
2 teaspoons curry paste
1 (14-oz.) can chopped tomatoes
1 teaspoon ground coriander
Grated peel and juice of 1/2 lemon
2 bay leaves
Freshly ground pepper
2/3 cup unsweetened coconut milk
Cilantro or lemon leaves, to garnish

Heat a wok until hot. Add oil and swirl to coat wok. Add gingerroot, garlic and chile and stir-fry 1 minute or until very fragrant. Add chicken pieces and stir-fry 3 or 4 minutes or until chicken begins to color. Stir in onion and curry paste and stir to coat. Add tomatoes and their juice, coriander, lemon peel, lemon juice, bay leaves and pepper. Bring to a simmer and cook 3 or 4 minutes or until sauce is slightly thickened.

Stir in coconut milk and reduce heat. Simmer 5 to 6 minutes or until sauce is thickened and chicken pieces are tender. Remove bay leaves and garnish with cilantro or lemon leaves. Serve with steamed basmati rice.

Makes 4 servings.

—SZECHUAN CHICKEN LIVERS—

1 ounce dried Chinese mushrooms or 4 ounces
   mushrooms, quartered
1 teaspoon Szechuan peppercorns
2 tablespoons vegetable oil
1 pound chicken livers, trimmed and cut in half
1-inch piece gingerroot, peeled and finely chopped
2 garlic cloves, finely chopped
4 to 6 green onions, thinly sliced
2 teaspoons cornstarch dissolved in 2 tablespoons
   water
2 tablespoons soy sauce
2 tablespoons rice wine or dry sherry
1/2 teaspoon sugar
Rice, to serve

If using dried mushrooms, place in a bowl, cover with warm water and soak 20 to 25 minutes. Using a slotted spoon, carefully remove mushrooms from water, to avoid disturbing any grit which has sunk to the bottom. Reserve liquid. Squeeze mushrooms dry, then cut off and discard stems. Heat wok until hot. Add Szechuan peppercorns and dry-fry 2 or 3 minutes or until very fragrant. Pour into a bowl to cool. When cold, crush in a mortar and pestle or grind in a spice grinder. Set aside.

Heat wok until hot. Add oil and swirl to coat wok. Pat livers dry and stir-fry 2 or 3 minutes. Add gingerroot, garlic, mushrooms and green onions. Stir-fry 2 minutes or until livers are brown. Add 2 tablespoons mushroom liquid if using dried mushrooms or 2 tablespoons water if using fresh mushrooms, to dissolved cornstarch. Stir cornstarch mixture, soy sauce, wine, ground peppercorns and sugar into wok. Cook, stirring, until thickened. Serve with rice.

Makes 4 servings.

—JAPANESE CHICKEN LIVERS—

2 tablespoons light soy sauce
2 tablespoons mirin or dry sherry mixed with 1/2
   teaspoon sugar
1 pound chicken livers, trimmed and cut in half
2 tablespoons vegetable oil
1 green bell pepper, diced
4 green onions, sliced
1 garlic clove, finely chopped
1-inch piece gingerroot, peeled and finely chopped
1/4 teaspoon red (cayenne) pepper
2 tablespoons sugar
3 tablespoons dark soy sauce
1 teaspoon sesame oil
Julienne strips of radish, to garnish (optional)

In a shallow dish, combine light soy sauce, mirin and chicken livers. Let marinate 20 to 30 minutes, stirring occasionally. Heat a wok until hot. Add oil and swirl to coat wok. With a slotted spoon, remove chicken livers from the marinade and add to wok. Stir-fry 3 or 4 minutes or until beginning to brown. Add bell pepper, green onions, garlic and gingerroot and stir-fry 1 or 2 minutes. The chicken livers should be browned, but still pink inside.

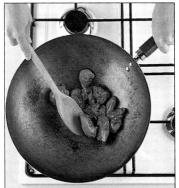

Stir in cayenne, sugar and dark soy sauce and toss to coat well. Drizzle with the sesame oil and serve immediately, garnished with radish, if desired.

Makes 4 servings.

DUCK WITH SPINACH

4 lean bacon slices, diced
1-1/2 pounds duck breast fillets, skinned and excess fat
    removed, cut crosswise into thin strips
1/2 pound shiitake mushrooms, sliced
1 garlic clove, finely chopped
1 onion, thinly sliced
2 tablespoons lemon juice
Salt and freshly ground pepper
5 tablespoons olive oil
1 pound fresh baby spinach leaves
2 tablespoons red-wine vinegar
1 teaspoon Dijon-style mustard
2 tablespoons pine nuts, toasted, to garnish

Place bacon in a cold wok. Heat wok over medium heat until bacon begins to release its fat. Stir-fry 2 or 3 minutes or until crisp. With a slotted spoon, remove to a bowl. Increase heat. Add duck strips to bacon fat in wok, working in 2 batches if necessary, and stir-fry 3 to 5 minutes or until brown and crisp. Remove to same bowl. Pour off all but 1 tablespoon fat from wok and add mushrooms, garlic, onion and lemon juice. Stir-fry 2 or 3 minutes or until liquid has evaporated. Remove to bowl, season and mix well. Wipe wok dry.

Add 1 tablespoon of the olive oil to wok and swirl to coat wok. Add spinach and stir-fry 1 minute or until spinach just wilts and turns bright green. Divide among 4 dinner plates. Pour remaining oil into wok, add the vinegar and mustard and stir to blend. Pour the liquid over the duck mixture in bowl and toss well to mix. Spoon equal amounts of duck mixture over the spinach on each plate and sprinkle with toasted pine nuts.

Makes 4 servings.

DUCK IN GINGER SAUCE

3 tablespoons olive oil
1 onion, chopped, and 5 garlic cloves, chopped
2-inch piece of gingerroot, peeled and sliced
1 tablespoon all-purpose flour
1/2 cup red wine
1 cup port
3 or 4 sprigs each thyme and rosemary
2 bay leaves
1 tablespoon black peppercorns
3 cups veal, duck or chicken stock
1-1/2 pounds duck breast fillets, skinned and excess fat
    removed, cut crosswise into thin strips
1 pound shiitake mushrooms, sliced
1/2 cup raisins
6 green onions, cut into 2-inch pieces
1 pound pappardelle or wide egg noodles

Heat wok until hot. Add 2 tablespoons of the oil and swirl to coat wok. Add onion, garlic and gingerroot and stir-fry 2 or 3 minutes or until onion is softened. Stir in flour until completely blended. Slowly pour in wine; cook, stirring, until thickened and blended. Add port, thyme, rosemary, bay leaves, peppercorns and stock. Bring to a boil and skim any foam which comes to the surface. Simmer, stirring often, 15 to 20 minutes or until lightly thickened and reduced by about half. Strain into a bowl.

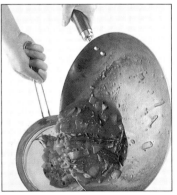

Wipe wok and heat until very hot, but not smoking. Add remaining oil and swirl to coat wok. Add duck strips and cook 2 or 3 minutes or until browned. Remove to a bowl. Stir in mushrooms, raisins and green onions and stir-fry 2 or 3 minutes. Add strained sauce and bring to a simmer. Add cooked duck. Cook pappardelle according to package directions. Drain and place in a large serving dish. Toss with sauce and duck.

Makes 4 servings.

—DUCK WITH BEETS & BEANS—

1 tablespoon olive oil
2 large duck breast fillets, 1/2 pound each, fat removed
 and skin left on
4 shallots, finely chopped
1 garlic clove, finely sliced
12 ounces shiitake mushrooms
1 tablespoon all-purpose flour
2 tablespoons fruity red wine
2/3 cup duck stock or chicken stock
1/2 pound fresh or frozen broad beans or lima beans
1 tablespoon red currant jelly
Freshly ground pepper
1 teaspoon cornstarch
1/2 teaspoon dry mustard powder
Grated peel and juice of 1 large orange
1 pound fresh baby beets, cooked and peeled

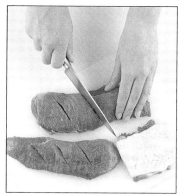

Heat wok until hot. Add oil and swirl to coat.
With a sharp knife, remove skin and make 2
or 3 diagonal slashes 1/2 inch deep across
duck breasts. Add to wok and cook over
medium heat 5 to 6 minutes or until
browned, turning. Remove to a plate and
keep warm. Add shallots and garlic to wok.
Stir-fry 1 minute, then add mushrooms and
stir-fry 2 or 3 minutes. Add flour and stir to
blend. Add wine and stock and bring to a
boil. Add beans.

Simmer, covered, 15 to 20 minutes or until
beans are tender and sauce is thickened, (if
using frozen beans, add 5 minutes before end
of cooking time). Stir in red currant jelly and
season with pepper. Meanwhile, in a saucepan, combine cornstarch, mustard powder,
orange peel, orange juice and beets. Boil 1
minute or until glaze thickens and beets are
heated through. Slice duck breasts thinly,
arrange slices on 4 dinner plates with beans
and beets.

Makes 4 servings.

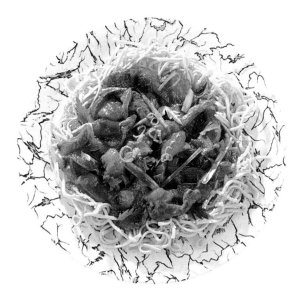

DUCK WITH PLUMS

2 tablespoons vegetable oil
1-1/2 pounds duck breast fillets, skinned and excess fat
    removed, cut crosswise into thin strips
1/2 pound red plums, pitted and thinly sliced
1/4 cup port
6 teaspoons red-wine vinegar
Grated peel and juice of 1 orange
2 tablespoons Chinese plum sauce or duck sauce
4 green onions, cut into thin strips
1 tablespoon soy sauce
3 or 4 whole cloves
Small piece cinnamon stick
1/2 teaspoon Chinese chili sauce or to taste
Parsley and grated orange peel, to garnish

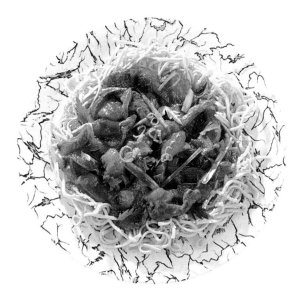

Heat a wok until hot. Add oil and swirl to coat wok. Add duck strips and stir-fry 3 or 4 minutes or until browned. Remove to a bowl. Add plums, port, vinegar, orange peel, orange juice, plum sauce, green onions, soy sauce, cloves, cinnamon stick and chili sauce to taste. Simmer 4 or 5 minutes or until plums begin to soften.

Return duck strips to wok and stir-fry 2 minutes or until duck is heated through and sauce is thickened. Garnish with parsley and grated orange peel. Serve with noodles.

Makes 4 servings.

TURKEY CHILI

1-1/2 pounds small turkey thighs
2 or 3 tablespoons vegetable oil
1 onion, chopped
4 garlic cloves, finely chopped
1 or 2 fresh hot red chiles, seeded and chopped
4 teaspoons chili powder
Red (cayenne) pepper, to taste
1-1/2 teaspoons ground cumin
1 (14-oz.) can peeled tomatoes
1-1/2 teaspoons brown sugar
Salt
2 (14-oz.) cans red kidney beans
Dairy sour cream and chopped fresh parsley, to garnish

With a small, sharp knife, remove skin from thighs and discard. Slice meat from thigh bones; cut into small pieces. Heat a wok until hot. Add 1 tablespoon of the oil and swirl to coat wok. Add half the turkey meat and stir-fry 4 or 5 minutes or until brown. Remove to a bowl; repeat with remaining turkey meat, adding a little more oil if necessary. Remove meat to bowl. Add remaining oil to wok and add onion and garlic. Stir-fry 3 or 4 minutes or until onion softens. Stir in chile, chili powder, cayenne and cumin.

Stir in tomatoes with their liquid, then add the sugar and season with salt. Add turkey and kidney beans to wok. Bring mixture to a boil and reduce heat. Simmer, covered, 45 to 55 minutes. Remove cover and cook 15 minutes more or until chili is thick. Taste and adjust seasoning, if necessary. Garnish with sour cream and chopped parsley and serve with rice.

Makes 6 to 8 servings.

——CREAMY TURKEY & PEAR——

2 tablespoons olive oil
1-1/2 pounds turkey cutlets
1 garlic clove, finely chopped
4 green onions, thinly sliced
1 tablespoon green peppercorns
1/4 cup brandy or white wine
1/2 cup whipping cream
1/2 teaspoon salt
1 pear or apple, cored and cut lengthwise into thin slices
Toasted sliced almonds and fresh chives, to garnish
Cooked snow peas, to serve

Heat a wok until hot. Add oil; swirl to coat wok. Arrange cutlets on bottom and up side of wok in a single layer, working in 2 batches.

Cook 3 to 5 minutes, turning once. Remove to a serving plate and keep warm. Add garlic, green onions and green peppercorns to wok and stir-fry 1 minute or until onions begin to soften. Add brandy and stir to deglaze. Cook 1 or 2 minutes to reduce slightly.

Stir in whipping cream and salt and bring to a boil. Reduce heat and add pear slices. Cook, covered, 1 or 2 minutes or until fruit slices are heated through, then arrange them over turkey cutlets. Pour sauce over and sprinkle with toasted almonds and chives. Serve with snow peas.

Makes 4 servings.

——— TURKEY MARSALA ———

1/3 cup sweet Marsala
3 tablespoons raisins
2 tablespoons butter
4 leeks (pale green and white parts only), cut in half
    lengthwise and sliced
1 cup chicken stock
1 bay leaf
1/2 teaspoon dried leaf thyme
1/4 teaspoon dried rubbed sage
1-1/4 pounds turkey cutlets, cut into strips
Finely grated peel of 1 lemon
2 teaspoons all-purpose flour
2 tablespoons whipping cream
Fresh sage leaves and lemon slices, to garnish
Orzo pasta, to serve

In a small bowl, combine Marsala and raisins. Let stand 20 minutes. Heat a wok until hot. Add 1 tablespoon of the butter and swirl to melt and coat wok. Add leeks and stir-fry 1 minute. Add 1/3 cup of the chicken stock, the bay leaf, thyme and sage and cook, covered, 4 to 6 minutes or until leeks are tender and liquid has evaporated. Discard bay leaf. Remove to a bowl and cover to keep warm. Wipe wok dry. Add remaining butter to wok and swirl to coat.

Add turkey, in 2 batches, and stir-fry for 2 minutes. Remove to a plate. Stir lemon peel and flour into remaining butter; cook 1 minute. Stir in remaining stock; bring to a boil. Add Marsala, raisins and cream; simmer 2 minutes. Spoon leek mixture onto plates, top with turkey and sauce. Garnish with sage and lemon. Serve with rice.

Makes 4 servings.

TURKEY WITH APPLE

1-1/2 pounds turkey cutlets, cut into strips
3 or 4 tablespoons seasoned all-purpose flour
3 or 4 tablespoons vegetable oil
1/3 cup chicken stock
2 tablespoons cider vinegar
1/2 teaspoon chili powder
Red (cayenne) pepper to taste
2 or 3 plum tomatoes, peeled, seeded and chopped
1 red onion, finely chopped
1 fresh hot red chile, seeded and chopped
1 Golden Delicious apple, cored and chopped
Cooked spinach noodles, to serve
2 tablespoons chopped fresh cilantro
1 tablespoon chopped peanuts

Dredge turkey strips in the seasoned flour.

Heat a wok until hot. Add 2 tablespoons of the oil and swirl to coat wok. Add half the turkey strips and stir-fry 1 or 2 minutes. Remove turkey to a serving plate; keep warm. Add 1 or 2 tablespoons of the remaining oil and cook remaining strips. Remove to the platter and keep warm.

Add stock and stir to deglaze wok. Add vinegar, chili powder, cayenne, tomatoes, onion, chile and chopped apple. Cook 1 or 2 minutes or until sauce thickens. Return turkey strips to wok and stir them into the sauce. Spoon over noodles. Sprinkle with cilantro and nuts.

Makes 4 servings.

CREAMY PAPRIKA TURKEY

4 tablespoons butter
1 onion, finely chopped
1 teaspoon paprika
1 cup whipping cream
1 tablespoon Dijon-style mustard
2 tablespoons chopped fresh dill
Salt and freshly ground pepper
1-1/2 pounds turkey cutlets, cut crosswise into
    1-inch strips
6 tablespoons seasoned all-purpose flour
2 tablespoons vegetable oil
1/2 pound tagliatelle or egg noodles
10 ounces fresh or frozen peas
2 teaspoons caraway seeds
Fresh dill sprigs, to garnish

Heat wok until hot. Add 1 tablespoon of the butter and swirl to coat wok. Add onion and stir-fry 7 or 8 minutes. Add paprika and cook 1 minute. Add cream and bring to a simmer; cook 1 or 2 minutes or until slightly thickened. Add mustard and dill and season with salt and pepper. Pour into a small bowl; keep warm. Wipe wok clean. Dredge turkey strips in seasoned flour. Heat a wok until hot. Add vegetable oil and 1 tablespoon butter and swirl to coat wok. Add turkey strips, working in batches and stir-fry 2 or 3 minutes. Remove to a plate and keep warm.

Cook tagliatelle according to package directions; drain well. Heat a wok until hot. Add remaining butter, peas and caraway seeds. Stir-fry 2 or 3 minutes or until peas are tender. Stir in noodles and season. Stir in a spoon of the reserved sauce and toss to coat noodles. Turn out onto serving plate. Pour remaining sauce and turkey strips into a wok, tossing to coat. Cook 1 minute. Spoon turkey strips and sauce over noodles. Garnish with dill sprigs.

Makes 4 servings.

—— TURKEY WITH BROCCOLI ——

1 tablespoon vegetable oil
1 pound turkey cutlets, cut into thin strips
1 tablespoon sesame oil
1 pound broccoli, stems and flowerets cut into
   1-inch pieces
4 green onions, cut into 1-inch pieces
1-inch piece gingerroot, peeled and cut into julienne
   strips
2 garlic cloves, finely chopped
1/4 cup dry sherry or rice wine
2 tablespoons light soy sauce
2 teaspoons cornstarch dissolved in 1 tablespoon water
1/4 cup chicken stock
1 (8-oz.) can water chestnuts, rinsed and sliced
Cilantro, to garnish
Cooked white rice and wild rice, to serve

Heat a wok until very hot but not smoking.
Add vegetable oil and swirl to coat wok. Add
turkey strips and stir-fry 2 or 3 minutes or
until beginning to color. Remove to a bowl.
Add sesame oil to wok. Add broccoli and stir-
fry 2 minutes. Add green onions, gingerroot
and garlic and stir-fry 2 or 3 minutes more or
until broccoli is tender but still crisp.

Add sherry and soy sauce and cook 2 minutes.
Stir dissolved cornstarch and chicken stock
together; stir into wok. Stir-fry 1 minute or
until sauce bubbles and thickens. Add
reserved turkey strips and water chestnuts,
tossing to coat, and cook 1 minute or until
turkey is heated through. Garnish with
cilantro and serve with rice.

Makes 4 servings.

——TURKEY WITH APRICOTS——

2 tablespoons olive oil
1-1/2 pounds turkey cutlets
1/2 teaspoon dried leaf thyme
Salt and freshly ground pepper
4 shallots, thinly sliced
3 tablespoons cranberries
1/4 cup dried apricots, chopped
1 small green bell pepper, diced
2 tablespoons cider vinegar
1/4 cup dry white wine or apple juice
1/2 cup chicken stock
1 or 2 tablespoons apricot preserves
1 tablespoon honey
Chopped fresh parsley or thyme, to garnish
Wild rice, to serve

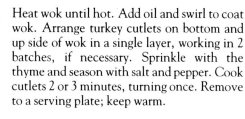

Heat wok until hot. Add oil and swirl to coat wok. Arrange turkey cutlets on bottom and up side of wok in a single layer, working in 2 batches, if necessary. Sprinkle with the thyme and season with salt and pepper. Cook cutlets 2 or 3 minutes, turning once. Remove to a serving plate; keep warm.

Add shallots, cranberries, apricots and bell pepper and stir-fry 1 minute. Stir in vinegar, wine, stock, apricot preserves and honey. Bring to a boil, reduce heat and simmer 3 or 4 minutes or until sauce thickens slightly and fruit is tender. Spoon sauce and fruit over turkey cutlets and garnish with parsley or thyme. Serve with wild rice.

Makes 4 servings.

SPICY SESAME BEEF

1 tablespoon cornstarch
3 tablespoons light soy sauce
1 pound beef sirloin steak, cut crosswise into thin strips
12 ounces broccoli
2 tablespoons sesame oil
1-inch piece gingerroot, peeled and cut into julienne
   strips
2 garlic cloves, finely chopped
1 fresh hot red chile, seeded and thinly sliced
1 red bell pepper, thinly sliced
1 (14-oz.) can baby corn on-the-cob, drained
1/2 cup beef stock, chicken stock or water
4 to 6 green onions, cut into 2-inch pieces
Toasted sesame seeds, to garnish
Noodles or rice, to serve

In a bowl, combine cornstarch and soy sauce. Add beef strips and toss to coat well. Let stand 20 minutes. Cut large flowerets from the broccoli and divide into small flowerets. With a vegetable peeler, peel the stalk and cut diagonally into 1-inch pieces. Heat a wok until very hot. Add sesame oil and swirl to coat. Add beef strips and marinade and stir-fry 2 or 3 minutes or until browned.

With a slotted spoon, remove beef strips to a bowl. Add gingerroot, garlic and chile to the wok and stir-fry 1 minute. Add broccoli, bell pepper and baby corn and stir-fry 2 or 3 minutes or until broccoli is tender but still crisp. Add the stock and stir 1 minute or until sauce bubbles and thickens. Add green onions and reserved beef strips and stir-fry 1 or 2 minutes or until beef strips are heated through. Sprinkle with sesame seeds and serve with noodles or rice.

Makes 4 servings.

TERIYAKA STEAKS

1/4 cup mirin or dry sherry sweetened with
   1 teaspoon sugar
1/4 cup light soy sauce
1/2-inch piece gingerroot, peeled and minced
1 garlic clove, finely chopped
1 teaspoon sugar
1/2 teaspoon red pepper sauce or to taste
4 beef sirloin or tenderloin steaks, cut into strips
2 tablespoons sesame oil
4 green onions, thinly sliced
Cilantro leaves, to garnish
Marinated cucumbers and rice, to serve

In a shallow baking dish, combine mirin, soy sauce, gingerroot, garlic, sugar and red pepper sauce to taste.

Add the meat and turn to coat well. Let stand 1 hour, turning strips once or twice.

Heat a wok until very hot. Add sesame oil and swirl to coat wok. Drain meat, reserving marinade, and add to wok. Stir-fry 2 or 3 minutes or until browned on all sides. Add marinade and green onions. Cook 3 to 5 minutes or until meat is cooked to desired doneness and most of marinade has evaporated, glazing the meat. Garnish with cilantro and serve with marinated cucumbers and rice.

Makes 4 servings.

——SPICY BEEF WITH PEPPERS——

1 tablespoon cornstarch
1/4 cup water
1/4 cup light soy sauce
1 tablespoon honey or brown sugar
1 teaspoon Chinese chili sauce
2 tablespoons vegetable oil
1 pound beef round or sirloin steak, cut crosswise into
   thin strips
1 tablespoon sesame oil
2 garlic cloves, finely chopped
1 fresh hot red chile, seeded and thinly sliced
1 onion, thinly sliced
1 each red, green and yellow bell pepper, cut into
   thin strips
Rice, to serve

In a small bowl, dissolve cornstarch in the water. Stir in soy sauce, honey and chili sauce until blended. Set aside. Heat a wok until very hot. Add vegetable oil and swirl to coat wok. Add beef strips and stir-fry 2 or 3 minutes or until beef is browned. With a slotted spoon, remove beef to a bowl.

Add sesame oil to the wok and add garlic and chile. Stir-fry 1 minute or until fragrant. Add onion and bell pepper strips and stir-fry 2 or 3 minutes or until beginning to soften. Stir cornstarch mixture, then stir into mixture in wok and stir until sauce bubbles and begins to thicken. Add beef strips and any juices and stir-fry 1 minute or until beef is heated through. Serve with rice.

Makes 4 servings.

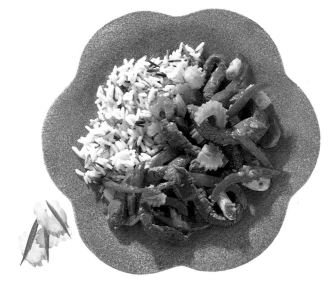

BEEF IN OYSTER SAUCE

1 tablespoon cornstarch
1-1/2 tablespoons soy sauce
1-1/2 tablespoons rice wine or dry sherry
1 pound beef round, sirloin or tenderloin steak, cut
   crosswise into thin strips
2 tablespoons sesame oil
1/2-inch piece gingerroot, peeled and chopped
2 garlic cloves, finely chopped
4 stalks celery, sliced
1 red bell pepper sliced
4 ounces mushrooms, sliced
4 green onions, sliced
2 tablespoons oyster sauce
1/2 cup chicken stock or water
White and wild rice mixture, to serve

In a bowl, combine 2 teaspoons of the corn-starch with soy sauce and sherry. Add beef strips and toss to coat well. Let stand 25 minutes. Heat a wok until very hot. Add oil and swirl to coat wok. Add beef strips and stir-fry 2 or 3 minutes or until browned. With a slotted spoon, remove to a bowl. Add gingerroot and garlic to oil remaining in wok and stir-fry 1 minute. Add celery, bell pepper, mushrooms and green onions and stir-fry 2 or 3 minutes or until vegetables begin to soften.

Stir in oyster sauce and combine remaining cornstarch with the stock, then stir into mixture in wok and bring to a boil. Add reserved beef strips and cook, stirring, 1 minute or until sauce bubbles and thickens and beef is heated through. Serve with rice.

Makes 4 servings.

───── DRY-FRIED BEEF STRIPS ─────

2 tablespoons sesame oil
1 pound beef round or sirloin steak, cut crosswise into
   julienne strips
2 tablespoons rice wine or dry sherry
1 tablespoon light soy sauce
2 garlic cloves, finely chopped
1/2-inch piece gingerroot, peeled and finely chopped
1 tablespoon Chinese hot bean sauce
2 teaspoons sugar
1 carrot, cut into julienne strips
2 celery stalks, cut into julienne strips
2 or 3 green onions, thinly sliced
1/4 teaspoon ground Szechuan pepper
White and wild rice mixture, to serve

Heat a wok until very hot. Add oil and swirl
to coat wok. Add beef and stir-fry 15 seconds
to quickly seal meat. Add 1 tablespoon of the
rice wine and stir-fry 1 or 2 minutes or until
beef is browned. Pour off and reserve any
excess liquid and continue stir-frying until
beef is dry.

Stir in soy sauce, garlic, gingerroot, bean
sauce, sugar, remaining rice wine and any
reserved cooking juices and stir to blend well.
Add carrot, celery, green onions and ground
Szechuan pepper and stir-fry until the vegetables begin to soften and all the liquid is
absorbed. Serve with rice.

Makes 4 servings.

— THAI BEEF WITH NOODLES —

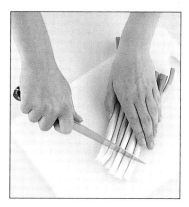

1/4 cup rice wine or dry sherry
2 tablespoons light soy sauce
2 garlic cloves, finely chopped
1-inch piece fresh gingerroot, peeled and finely
    chopped
1/2 teaspoon dried crushed chiles
1 pound sirloin or tenderloin steak, 1-inch thick, cut
    crosswise into 1/2-inch strips
12 ounces ramen noodles or thin spaghetti
1 tablespoon sesame oil
4 ounces snow peas
4 to 6 green onions, cut into 2-inch pieces
2 teaspoons cornstarch, dissolved in 1/4 cup water
2 tablespoons chopped cilantro
Cilantro leaves and lime slices, to garnish

In a shallow baking dish, combine rice wine,
soy sauce, garlic, gingerroot and chiles. Add
steak to dish and marinate 30 minutes,
covered, turning once. Cook noodles according to package directions, drain and set aside.
Heat wok until very hot. Add sesame oil and
swirl to coat wok. Remove steak from marinade, scraping off any gingerroot and garlic
and reserving marinade. Pat steak dry with
paper towels. Add steak to wok and stir-fry 4
minutes or until browned. Remove and keep
warm.

Add snow peas and green onions to any oil
remaining in wok and stir-fry 1 minute. Stir
cornstarch mixture and stir into wok with
reserved marinade Bring to a boil, stirring.
Add reserved noodles and chopped cilantro.
Add beef. Toss to coat well. Divide among 4
plates. Garnish with cilantro leaves and lime
slices.

Makes 4 servings.

─── BEEF STROGANOFF ───

2 tablespoons peanut oil and 1 tablespoon butter
1 pound beef tenderloin or boneless sirloin steak, cut
   crosswise into 1/2-inch strips
1 onion, thinly sliced
1/2 pound mushrooms, thinly sliced
Salt and freshly ground black pepper
1 tablespoon all-purpose flour
1/2 cup beef stock or veal stock
1 tablespoon Dijon-style mustard (optional)
1 cup dairy sour cream
2 tablespoons chopped dill
Pinch of red (cayenne) pepper
Rice, to serve

Heat a wok until very hot. Add oil and swirl to coat wok. Add half of the beef strips.

Stir-fry 1 minute or until just browned and still pink in center. With a slotted spoon, remove beef to a bowl. Reheat wok and add remaining beef strips. Stir-fry 1 minute and turn beef and any juices into bowl. Add butter to wok, then add onion. Reduce heat to medium and stir-fry onion 3 or 4 minutes or until softened and beginning to color. Add mushrooms and increase heat; stir-fry 2 minutes or until mushrooms and onions are softened and golden. Add salt and pepper and stir in flour until well-blended.

Add beef broth and bring to a boil, then simmer 1 minute or until sauce thickens. Stir in mustard, if using, and gradually add the sour cream. (Do not allow sour cream to boil.) Return beef strips and any juices to sauce, stir in chopped dill and simmer 1 minute or until beef is heated through. Sprinkle a little cayenne. Serve with rice.

Makes 6 servings.

—MEXICAN BEEF WITH BEANS—

1 pound ground beef
1 onion, chopped
3 or 4 garlic cloves, finely chopped
1 green or red bell pepper, diced
1 (4-oz.) can chopped green chiles, drained
1 (14-oz.) can red kidney beans, drained
1 (11-1/2-oz.) can whole-kernel corn, drained
2 tablespoons chili powder or to taste
2 teaspoons ground cumin
1 teaspoon dried leaf oregano
1 (28-oz.) can peeled tomatoes
Salt and freshly ground black pepper
3 tablespoons chopped fresh parsley
1 cup shredded sharp Cheddar cheese

In a wok, place beef and heat until it begins to release juices. Increase heat and stir to break up meat and stir-fry 5 or 6 minutes or until meat is browned. Add onion, garlic, bell pepper, chopped chiles, kidney beans and corn and bring to a boil.

Stir in chili powder, cumin, oregano and peeled tomatoes with their juice. Stir to break up tomatoes. Season with salt and pepper, reduce heat and cook, covered, 20 to 30 minutes or until slightly thickened. Remove from heat, stir in parsley and half of the cheese. Sprinkle with remaining cheese.

Makes 6 to 8 servings.

ITALIAN BEEF SALAD

1 small head of Romaine lettuce, dried thoroughly
2 or 3 tablespoons olive oil
1 pound beef tenderloin steak, frozen 20 minutes, then
    cut into very thin strips
8 anchovy fillets, sliced if large
2 ounces Parmesan cheese
2 to 4 tablespoons lemon juice
1 tablespoon capers, rinsed and drained
Salt and freshly ground pepper
Chopped herbs, to garnish

Arrange the Romaine leaves on 4 large plates. Set aside.

Heat wok until very hot. Add 1 tablespoon of the olive oil and a few beef strips. Stir-fry 5 to 8 seconds or until beef just colors. The beef should be very rare. Remove to one of the salad plates. Continue cooking beef in batches, adding oil as necessary, and arranging cooked beef over leaves.

Place a few anchovy slices over the beef slices. Using a vegetable peeler, shave paper-thin slices of Parmesan cheese over the meat. Drizzle each salad with lemon juice and sprinkle with capers. Season with salt and pepper. Garnish with herbs.

Makes 4 servings.

——— VEAL WITH PINE NUTS ———

1/2 pound veal cutlets
3 tablespoons all-purpose flour
Salt and freshly ground pepper
2 slices bacon, diced
4 tablespoons butter
2 tablespoons pine nuts
1/2 cup dry white wine
1 tablespoon capers, drained
2 teaspoons shredded fresh sage leaves
Sage leaves, to garnish (optional)
Linguine, to serve

Place cutlets between 2 sheets of waxed paper and pound to 1/2 inch thickness. Cut veal into strips.

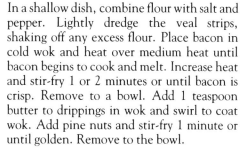

In a shallow dish, combine flour with salt and pepper. Lightly dredge the veal strips, shaking off any excess flour. Place bacon in cold wok and heat over medium heat until bacon begins to cook and melt. Increase heat and stir-fry 1 or 2 minutes or until bacon is crisp. Remove to a bowl. Add 1 teaspoon butter to drippings in wok and swirl to coat wok. Add pine nuts and stir-fry 1 minute or until golden. Remove to the bowl.

Add 1 tablespoon butter and the veal strips and stir-fry 2 or 3 minutes or until golden on all sides. Remove veal to 2 dinner plates and keep warm. Add wine to wok, stirring to deglaze and bring to a boil. Boil 1 or 2 minutes or until reduced by half, then stir in remaining butter. Add capers, bacon, pine nuts and shredded sage and toss well. Season with pepper and spoon over veal. Garnish with sage leaves, if using. Serve with linguine.

Makes 2 servings.

—VEAL IN MUSTARD CREAM—

3 tablespoons all-purpose flour
Salt and red (cayenne) pepper
1/2 pound veal cutlets
1 tablespoon vegetable oil
1 tablespoon butter
2 or 3 shallots, thinly sliced
1/4 cup dry white wine
1/2 cup whipping cream
2 tablespoons Dijon-style mustard
2 tablespoons fresh basil leaves or small dill sprigs with
   a few reserved garnish

In a shallow dish, combine flour with salt and cayenne to taste.

Place veal cutlets between 2 sheets of waxed paper and pound to 1/4 inch thickness. Cut veal into strips. Lightly dredge the veal strips, shaking off any excess flour. Heat a wok until very hot. Add the oil and swirl to coat wok. Add butter and swirl. Add veal strips and stir-fry 2 or 3 minutes or until golden on all sides. Remove veal to 2 dinner plates and keep warm.

Add shallots to remaining oil in wok and cook 2 or 3 minutes or until softened. Add wine, stirring to deglaze, and bring to a boil. Boil 1 or 2 minutes or until reduced by half, then stir in cream and bring back to a boil. Cook 1 minute or until sauce thickens slightly. Stir in the mustard and basil. Pour sauce over veal and garnish with reserved basil. Serve with linguine or fried potatoes.

Makes 2 servings.

—CALVES LIVER WITH BACON—

4 slices bacon, cut into pieces
1 onion, thinly sliced lengthwise into 'petals'
1 Granny Smith apple, cored and thinly sliced
Salt and freshly ground pepper
1 tablespoon vegetable oil
12 ounces calves liver, cut into thin strips
2 tablespoons cider vinegar
1/4 cup dry white wine or apple juice
2 teaspoons cornstarch, dissolved in 1/4 cup chicken
　　stock or water
1/2 teaspoon dried leaf thyme
Thyme sprigs or lemon wedges, to garnish

Place bacon in a cold wok and heat over medium heat until bacon begins to cook.

Increase heat and stir-fry 1 or 2 minutes or until bacon is crisp. Remove to a bowl. Add onion to dripping in wok and stir-fry 1 or 2 minutes or until just beginning to soften. Add apple slices and stir-fry 1 or 2 minutes or until apple begins to soften. Season with salt and pepper and remove to bowl. Add oil to wok and increase heat. Add liver strips and stir-fry 1 or 2 minutes or until just browned. The liver should be pink inside. Remove to bowl.

Stir cider vinegar into wok to deglaze, then stir in wine. Stir cornstarch mixture and stir into wok with the thyme. Add reserved bacon, onion, apple and liver strips and cook 1 minute or until sauce bubbles and liver is heated through. Garnish with thyme sprigs or lemon wedge and serve with mashed potatoes.

Makes 2 servings.

LAMB WITH TOMATOES

1 tablespoon olive oil
4 (1/2-inch-thick) lamb leg steaks or sirloin chops,
    about 6 ounces each
2 garlic cloves, chopped
1 small hot red chile, seeded and chopped
1 green bell pepper, diced
1 zucchini, sliced
1/2 pound red or red and yellow cherry tomatoes
1/3 cup sun-dried tomatoes in oil, drained and chopped
2 tablespoons bottled pesto sauce
Basil sprigs, to garnish

Heat a wok until very hot. Add the olive oil
and swirl to coat.

Add the lamb and reduce heat slightly, then
cook 3 to 5 minutes or until browned on both
sides, turning once halfway through cooking.
The lamb should be pink inside. Remove and
keep warm. Pour off all but 1 tablespoon oil
from wok and add garlic, chile and bell
pepper. Stir-fry 1 minute.

Add zucchini, cherry tomatoes, sun-dried
tomatoes and pesto sauce and stir-fry 3 or 4
minutes, or until vegetables are tender but
still crisp. Push vegetables aside and return
lamb to wok. Cover lamb with vegetables and
cook lamb and vegetables together 1 minute
until flavors blend and lamb is heated
through. Serve 1 or 2 steaks or chops per
person, garnished with basil.

Makes 2 or 4 servings.

——LAMB WITH SPINACH——

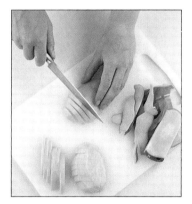

3 tablespoons soy sauce
1/4 teaspoon five-spice powder
1-inch piece gingerroot, peeled and cut into julienne
  strips
2 garlic cloves, finely chopped
1-1/2 pounds lean lamb, cut into thin strips
1 tablespoon sesame oil
1 fresh hot red chile, seeded and thinly sliced
8 green onions, cut into 2-inch pieces
1 mango, peeled and cut into 1/2-inch-thick pieces
6 ounces fresh spinach leaves, washed and dried
3 tablespoons dry sherry or rice wine
1 teaspoon cornstarch dissolved in 1 tablespoon water

In a shallow baking dish, combine soy sauce, five-spice powder, gingerroot and garlic. Add lamb strips and toss to coat well. Marinate 1 hour, covered, stirring occasionally. Heat a wok until very hot. Add sesame oil and swirl to coat. With a slotted spoon and working in 2 batches, add lamb to wok, draining off and reserving as much marinade as possible. Stir-fry lamb 2 or 3 minutes or until browned on all sides. Remove to a bowl. Add chile to oil remaining in wok and stir-fry 1 minute.

Add green onions and mango and stir-fry 1 minute. Stir in spinach leaves, reserved lamb, sherry and reserved marinade. Stir cornstarch mixture and stir into wok. Stir-fry 1 minute, tossing all ingredients until spinach wilts and lamb is lightly glazed with sauce. Serve with noodles.

Makes 4 servings.

ORANGE-GLAZED LAMB

1 tablespoon vegetable oil
8 (1-inch-thick) boneless lean lamb chops about 1-1/2
   pounds total
2/3 cup dry white wine
2/3 cup freshly squeezed orange juice
1 teaspoon ground coriander
1/2 teaspoon dry mustard powder
Salt and freshly ground pepper
1 tablespoon cornstarch dissolved in 2 tablespoons
   water
1 large orange, peel removed and cut into julienne
   strips, and divided into segments
Fresh green beans, to serve

Heat a wok until very hot. Add vegetable oil
and swirl to coat wok.

Add lamb strips and stir-fry 4 or 5 minutes.
Remove to a plate and keep warm. Pour off all
the fat from the wok and add wine, stirring to
deglaze. Add orange juice, coriander,
mustard powder, salt and pepper and bring to
a boil. Stir the cornstarch mixture and slowly
pour into the wok, stirring constantly until
sauce thickens.

Return the lamb strips to the sauce and,
turning to coat, cook 1 or 2 minutes or until
sauce has glazed the lamb strips and they are
heated through. Add orange peel and orange
segments and cook 1 minute to heat through.
Arrange lamb mixture on 4 dinner plates.
Serve with green beans.

Makes 4 servings.

MEXICAN-STYLE LAMB

1/2 cup dry white wine
1/2 cup pineapple juice
2 to 4 tablespoons lime or lemon juice
1/2 cup fresh chopped cilantro
3 fresh hot red chiles, seeded and chopped
2 garlic cloves, finely chopped
1-1/2 pounds lean lamb, cut into thin strips
1 large avocado
1 large tomato, peeled, seeded and chopped
1 head Romaine lettuce, shredded
2 tablespoons vegetable oil
1 onion, sliced
6 warm tortillas or pita breads, to serve (optional)

In a medium-size bowl, combine 1 tablespoon each of the wine, pineapple juice and lime juice, 2 tablespoons of the cilantro, 1 of the chiles and half the chopped garlic. Set aside. Combine the remainder of these ingredients in a shallow baking dish and add the lamb strips. Toss to coat then marinate, covered, 1 hour. Chop avocado and add to the first bowl with the chopped tomato. Toss to blend ingredients. Arrange lettuce around edge of a serving plate, spoon avocado mixture on top and set aside.

Heat a wok until very hot. Add the oil and swirl to coat. With a slotted spoon, remove lamb strips from marinade and add to wok in 2 batches and stir-fry 2 or 3 minutes or until browned. Remove to a bowl. Add onion to the wok and stir-fry 2 or 3 minutes or until softened. Return lamb and any juices to the wok. Cook 1 minute or until lamb is heated through. Spoon lamb onto center of serving dish and serve with warm tortillas or pita bread, if desired.

Makes 6 servings.

STIR-FRIED MOUSSAKA

1 tablespoon olive oil
2 onions, chopped
2 garlic cloves, chopped
1-1/2 pounds lean ground lamb
1 (14-oz.) can chopped or crushed tomatoes
3 or 4 zucchini, sliced into 1/2-inch pieces
1 tablespoon capers, rinsed and drained
2 tablespoons chopped fresh oregano or basil or
    1 tablespoon dried leaf oregano or basil
Salt and freshly ground pepper
1-1/4 cups orzo
1 cup crumbled feta cheese
Green salad and crusty bread, to serve

Heat a wok until hot. Add oil and swirl to coat wok. Add onions and garlic and stir-fry 2 or 3 minutes or until softened. Add lamb and stir-fry 4 or 5 minutes or until browned.

Add tomatoes, zucchini, capers, oregano, salt and pepper. Stir in 1-1/2 cups water and the orzo and bring to a boil. Reduce heat to low and cook, covered, 8 to 10 minutes or until orzo is cooked and most of the liquid absorbed. Remove wok from heat and stir in the feta cheese. Serve with salad and crusty bread.

Makes 6 to 8 servings.

——— PORK & PRUNE MEDLEY ———

1 pound pork tenderloin, cut into thin slices
2 tablespoons soy sauce
2 tablespoons balsamic vinegar or cider vinegar
2 tablespoons olive oil
2 zucchini, sliced
1 onion, cut lengthwise into thin wedges
1 red bell pepper, cut into thin strips
4 ounces mushrooms, sliced
4 ounces snow peas
4 ounces asparagus, cut into 2-inch pieces
1/2 cup walnut halves
6 ounces pitted prunes
Salt and freshly ground black pepper

In a shallow baking dish, sprinkle pork slices with soy sauce and vinegar and toss to coat well. Let stand 30 minutes. Heat a wok until hot. Add olive oil and swirl to coat wok. Add pork slices and stir-fry 3 to 5 minutes, or until golden on all sides. With a slotted spoon, remove to a bowl.

Add zucchini, onion, bell pepper, mushrooms, snow peas, asparagus, walnut halves and prunes and stir-fry 2 or 3 minutes until coated with oil. Add 2 tablespoons water to wok and cover wok quickly. Steam 1 or 2 minutes or until vegetables just begin to soften. Uncover wok, return pork to wok and toss to mix. Season with salt and pepper. Stir-fry 1 or 2 minutes or until pork is heated through.

Makes 4 servings.

—COCONUT PORK WITH LIME—

6 pork cutlets, about 4 ounces each
1/2-inch piece gingerroot, peeled and grated
2 teaspoons ground cumin
1 teaspoon ground coriander
1 teaspoon chili powder to taste
1 teaspoon paprika
1/2 teaspoon salt
2 tablespoons vegetable oil
1 onion, cut lengthwise into thin wedges
3 or 4 garlic cloves, finely chopped
1-1/4 cups unsweetened coconut milk
Grated peel and juice of 1 large lime
1 small bok choy, shredded
Lime slices and cilantro leaves, to garnish
Noodles, to serve

Place cutlets between 2 sheets of waxed paper. Pound to 1/4 inch thickness. Cut pork into strips. In a large shallow dish, combine gingerroot, cumin, coriander, chili powder, paprika and salt. Stir in pork strips and let stand 15 minutes. Heat a wok until very hot. Add oil and swirl to coat wok. Add pork and stir-fry 2 or 3 minutes or until cooked through. Remove to a plate and keep warm. Pour off all but 1 tablespoon oil from the wok.

Add onion and garlic to wok and stir-fry 2 or 3 minutes or until onion is softened. Slowly add coconut milk. Bring to a simmer but do not boil. Stir in lime peel, lime juice and bok choy cabbage. Simmer 5 to 7 minutes, stirring frequently, or until bok choy is tender and sauce slightly thickened. Add pork and cook, covered, 1 or 2 minutes or until heated through. Arrange pork mixture on plates and garnish with lime slices and cilantro. Serve with noodles.

Makes 6 servings.

── RATATOUILLE-STYLE PORK ──

1 tablespoon olive oil
4 (1-inch-thick) boneless loin pork chops, about 1-1/4
    pounds total, trimmed of fat
1 onion, coarsely chopped
2 garlic cloves, chopped
1 small eggplant, cut into 1-inch cubes
1 red or green bell pepper, diced
2 zucchini, thickly sliced
1 (8-oz.) can chopped tomatoes
1 teaspoon chopped fresh oregano or basil or 1/2
    teaspoon dried leaf oregano or basil
1/2 teaspoon dried thyme leaves
Salt and freshly ground black pepper
Flat leaf parsley, to garnish
Fresh noodles, to serve

Heat a wok until very hot. Add olive oil and swirl to coat wok. Arrange pork chops on bottom and side of wok, in a single layer. Fry 4 or 5 minutes or until well browned on both sides, turning once and rotating during cooking. Remove to a plate. Add onion and garlic to remaining oil in wok and stir-fry 1 minute or until onion begins to soften. Add eggplant and bell pepper and stir-fry 3 to 5 minutes to brown and soften.

Add zucchini, chopped tomatoes and their juice, oregano, thyme and season with salt and pepper. Stir well and return pork chops to wok, covering them with the ratatouille mixture. Reduce heat and cook, covered, 6 to 8 minutes, shaking wok occasionally to prevent sticking. Uncover and cook 2 or 3 minutes to thicken sauce slightly. Garnish with parsley. Serve with noodles.

Makes 4 servings.

—— INDONESIAN-STYLE PORK ——

1 tablespoon all-purpose flour, seasoned
1-1/4 pounds pork tenderloin, cut into small cubes
2 or 3 tablespoons vegetable oil
1 onion, cut lengthwise in half and thinly sliced
2 garlic cloves, finely chopped
1-inch piece gingerroot, peeled and cut into julienne
  strips
1/2 teaspoon sambal oelek (see Note) or Chinese chili
  sauce
1/4 cup Indonesian soy sauce or dark soy sauce
  sweetened with 1 tablespoon sugar
Cilantro leaves, to garnish

In a bowl, combine seasoned flour and pork; toss to coat. Shake to remove excess flour.

Heat a wok until very hot. Add 2 tablespoons of the oil and swirl to coat wok. Add pork cubes and stir-fry 3 or 4 minutes or until browned on all sides, adding a little more oil if necessary. Push pork to one side and add onion, garlic and gingerroot and stir-fry 1 minute, tossing all the ingredients.

Add sambal oelek, soy sauce and 2/3 cup water; stir. Bring to a boil, then reduce heat to low and simmer, covered, 20 to 25 minutes, stirring occasionally, or until pork is tender and sauce thickened. Garnish with cilantro and serve with fried rice.

Makes 4 servings.

Note: Sambal oelek is a very hot, chile-based Indonesian condiment available in speciality or oriental food shops.

–PORK WITH MELON & MANGO–

1 small cantaloupe or 1/2 Honeydew melon, cut into thin strips
1 slightly under-ripe mango, peeled and cut into thin strips
Salt and freshly ground pepper
1 tablespoon sugar
Juice of 1 lime or lemon
2 tablespoons sesame oil
1/2 pound pork tenderloin, cut into shreds
4 to 6 green onions, thinly sliced
2 garlic cloves, finely chopped
5 tablespoons nam pla (fish sauce)
1 tablespoon cider vinegar
1/2 teaspoon crushed dried chiles
Chopped peanuts and chopped cilantro, to garnish

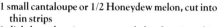

In a medium-size bowl, toss melon and mango strips with salt, pepper, sugar and lime juice. Set aside. Heat a wok until very hot. Add oil and swirl to coat wok, add shredded pork and stir-fry 2 or 3 minutes or until golden. With a slotted spoon, remove to paper towels and drain.

To the oil remaining in the wok, add green onions and garlic and stir-fry 1 minute. Stir in the nam pla, vinegar and crushed chiles. Add the reserved pork and the melon mixture, together with any juices. Toss to mix ingredients and heat through. Spoon onto a shallow serving dish and sprinkle with chopped peanuts and cilantro. Serve hot or warm with noodles or shredded Chinese cabbage.

Makes 2 servings.

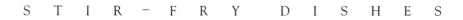

— CHINESE SAUSAGE STIR-FRY —

2 tablespoons sesame oil or vegetable oil
1/2 pound Chinese sausage (see Note) or sweet Italian-
    style sausage, cut diagonally into thin slices
1 onion, cut in half lengthwise and sliced
1 red bell pepper, diced
4 ounces canned baby corn-on-the-cobs
2 zucchini, thinly sliced
4 ounces snow peas
8 green onions, cut into 1-inch pieces
1 ounce bean sprouts, rinsed and drained
1/4 cup cashew nuts or peanuts
2 tablespoons soy sauce
3 tablespoons dry sherry or rice wine
Rice or noodles, to serve

Heat a wok until hot. Add oil and swirl to coat wok. Add sausage slices and stir-fry 3 or 4 minutes or until browned and cooked. Add onion, bell pepper and baby corn and stir-fry 3 minutes. Add zucchini, snow peas and green onions and stir-fry 2 minutes.

Stir in the bean sprouts and nuts and stir-fry 1 or 2 minutes. Add soy sauce and dry sherry and stir-fry 1 minute or until vegetables are tender but still crisp and sausage slices completely cooked through. Serve with rice or noodles.

Makes 4 servings.

Note: Chinese sausage is available in Chinese groceries and some speciality shops and must be cooked before eating.

SAUSAGE & PEPPERS

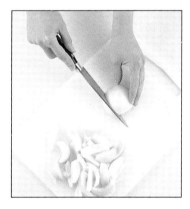

2 tablespoons olive oil
1-1/2 pounds hot, sweet or mixed Italian sausages
2 onions, halved lengthwise, then cut lengthwise into
    thin wedges
4 to 6 garlic cloves, finely chopped
1 each large red, green and yellow bell peppers, cut in
    half lengthwise, then into strips
1 (8-oz.) can peeled tomatoes
1 tablespoon shredded fresh oregano or basil or
    1 teaspoon dried leaf oregano or basil
1/2 teaspoon crushed dried chiles
1/2 teaspoon dried leaf thyme
1/2 teaspoon rubbed sage
Salt and freshly ground black pepper
Oregano or basil leaves, to garnish
Parmesan cheese, to garnish

Heat a wok until hot. Add olive oil and swirl to coat wok. Add sausages and cook over medium heat 8 to 10 minutes or until sausages are brown on all sides, turning and rotating sausages frequently during cooking. Remove sausages to a plate and pour off all but 2 tablespoons oil from the wok. Add onions and garlic and stir-fry 2 minutes or until golden. Add bell pepper strips and stir-fry 1 or 2 minutes or until just beginning to soften.

Add tomatoes and their liquid, oregano, crushed chiles, thyme, sage, salt and pepper. Stir to break up the tomatoes and mix well. Return sausages to wok and cover with the vegetable mixture. Simmer 15 to 20 minutes or until vegetables are tender and sauce is thickened. Garnish with oregano leaves and shaved or grated Parmesan cheese. Serve with spaghetti.

Makes 6 servings.

SPICY PORK WITH PEAS

1 pound pork tenderloin, cut crosswise into thin slices
1-1/2 tablespoons soy sauce
2 tablespoons cider vinegar
1 tablespoon vegetable oil
1-inch piece gingerroot, peeled and finely chopped
2 garlic cloves, finely chopped
1 fresh hot red chile, seeded and thinly sliced
1/2 pound fresh or frozen green peas or sugar snap peas
1 head radicchio or 1/2 head small red cabbage, thinly
    shredded
Rice pilaf, to serve

In a small baking dish, sprinkle pork slices
with soy sauce and vinegar. Toss to coat well.
Let stand 15 to 20 minutes.

Heat a wok until hot. Add oil and swirl to
coat wok. Add pork slices and stir-fry 2
minutes. Push to one side and add gingerroot,
garlic and chile and stir-fry 1 minute to mix.

Add peas and radicchio and stir-fry 2 or 3
minutes or until vegetables are tender but still
crisp. Serve with rice pilaf.

Makes 4 servings.

—PORK CUTLETS NORMANDY—

4 (1/2-inch-thick) pork cutlets, about 1-1/4 pounds
   total
2 tablespoons vegetable oil
2 tablespoons butter
1 garlic clove, chopped
2 Golden Delicious apples, cored and thinly sliced
1/2 teaspoon dried leaf thyme
3 tablespoons Calvados or brandy
1/2 cup whipping cream
Salt and freshly ground pepper
Flat-leaf parsley, to garnish

Place pork cutlets between 2 sheets of waxed
paper and pound to 1/4 inch thickness. Cut
into thin strips.

Heat a wok until very hot. Add oil and swirl
to coat wok. Add pork strips and stir-fry 3 or
4 minutes or until cooked through. Remove
to a plate and keep warm. Pour off any oil
from the wok. Add butter to the wok and
melt. Add garlic, apple slices and thyme and
stir-fry 1 or 2 minutes or until apple slices are
golden.

Add Calvados to the wok and stir to deglaze.
Add cream and bring to a boil. Add salt and
pepper to taste. Cook 1 minute, stirring
constantly, until sauce thickens slightly and
apples are tender. Arrange pork on a serving
dish. Garnish with parsley sprigs. Serve with
buttered egg noodles.

Makes 4 servings.

PORK WITH BASIL

9 ounces thin egg noodles
4 tablespoons olive oil
1-1/4 pounds pork tenderloin, cut into shreds
1 red onion, cut lengthwise in half, and thinly sliced
1/4 cup shredded fresh basil leaves
2 tablespoons balsamic vinegar
3 tablespoons pine nuts, toasted
Salt and freshly ground pepper
Basil leaves, to garnish

In a large saucepan of boiling water, cook egg noodles according to package directions. Drain, turn into a large bowl and toss with 2 tablespoons of the olive oil. Keep warm.

Heat a wok until very hot. Add remaining olive oil and swirl to coat wok. Add shredded pork and stir-fry 2 or 3 minutes or until pork is golden. Add onion and toss with the pork, then stir-fry 1 minute.

Stir in shredded basil, the balsamic vinegar and pine nuts and toss to mix well. Add noodles to the wok, season to taste and toss with pork mixture. Turn into shallow a serving dish and garnish with basil leaves.

Makes 4 servings.

—SPICY MEATBALLS & TOFU—

12 ounces lean ground pork
1 egg white
1 or 2 tablespoons chili sauce
1/2 teaspoon ground turmeric
Salt
3 tablespoons vegetable oil
1/2 pound firm tofu, drained and cubed
1 red bell pepper, diced
1/2 pound green beans, cut into 1-inch pieces
2 garlic cloves, finely chopped
1-inch piece gingerroot, peeled and finely chopped
2 teaspoons cornstarch
1/2 cup chicken stock
Flat-leaf parsley sprigs, to garnish
Rice, to serve

In a bowl, combine ground pork, egg white, 1/2 teaspoon of the chili sauce, turmeric and salt. Mix well. With your hands, form mixture into 16 small balls. Refrigerate 25 to 30 minutes to firm. Heat a wok until hot. Add 2 tablespoons of the oil and, working in 2 batches, add the pork balls. Stir-fry 3 or 4 minutes or until golden on all sides. Remove balls to paper towels to drain; keep warm. Add tofu cubes to wok and stir-fry gently 2 or 3 minutes, being careful tofu does not break up. With a slotted spoon, remove to paper towels to drain.

Add remaining oil to wok. Add bell pepper and beans and stir-fry 3 or 4 minutes. Remove to a bowl. Add garlic and gingerroot to wok and stir-fry 1 minute. Dissolve cornstarch in chicken stock and stir into wok. Add remaining chili sauce to taste and simmer, stirring, 1 minute. Return pork to wok and simmer, covered, 8 to 10 minutes. Uncover and add bean curd, bell pepper and beans. Cook gently 1 or 2 minutes. Garnish with parsley and serve with rice.

Makes 4 servings.

──── HAM & PLUM STIR-FRY ────

2 tablespoons vegetable oil
1 red bell pepper, cut lengthwise in half, thinly sliced
12 ounces plums or nectarines, thinly sliced
1/2 pound oyster mushrooms, sliced
2 leeks, trimmed, washed and cut diagonally into
   1/2-inch pieces
6 green onions, thinly sliced
1 pound ham steaks, cut into thin strips
1 cup orange juice
2 tablespoons peach or apricot preserve
2 tablespoons soy sauce
2 tablespoons white-wine vinegar
2 tablespoons cornstarch dissolved in 2 tablespoons
   water
Noodles or rice, to serve

Heat a wok until hot. Add oil and swirl to coat wok. Add bell pepper, and plums and stir-fry 1 or 2 minutes. Add oyster mushrooms and leeks and stir-fry 1 or 2 minutes or until vegetables begin to soften. Push vegetables to one side and add green onions and ham strips. Stir-fry 2 or 3 minutes, tossing ingredients to mix, or until ham is heated through.

Stir in orange juice, peach preserve, soy sauce and vinegar. Stir cornstarch mixture, then stir into wok. Bring to a boil and stir-fry 1 or 2 minutes or until sauce thickens and coats ingredients. Serve with noodles or rice.

Makes 4 to 6 servings.

SZECHUAN EGGPLANT

1 pound small eggplants, cut into 1-inch cubes or
   thin slices
Salt
2 tablespoons peanut oil
2 garlic cloves, finely chopped
1-inch piece gingerroot, peeled and finely chopped
3 or 4 green onions, finely sliced
2 tablespoons dark soy sauce
1 or 2 tablespoons hot bean sauce or 1 teaspoon crushed
   dried chiles
1 tablespoon yellow bean paste (optional)
2 tablespoons dry sherry or rice wine
1 tablespoon cider vinegar
1 tablespoon sugar
Chopped parsley, to garnish

Place eggplant cubes in a plastic or stainless
steel colander or sieve, placed on a plate or
baking sheet. Sprinkle with salt and let stand
30 minutes. Rinse eggplant under cold run-
ning water and turn out onto layers of paper
towels; pat dry thoroughly. Heat wok until
very hot. Add oil and swirl to coat wok. Add
garlic, gingerroot and green onions and stir-
fry 1 or 2 minutes or until green onions begin
to soften. Add eggplant and stir-fry 2 or 3
minutes or until softened and beginning to
brown.

Stir in remaining ingredients and 2/3 cup
water and bring to a boil. Reduce heat and
simmer 5 to 7 minutes or until eggplant is
very tender, stirring frequently. Increase heat
to high and stir-fry mixture until the liquid is
almost completely reduced. Spoon into a
serving dish and garnish with parsley.

Makes 4 to 6 servings.

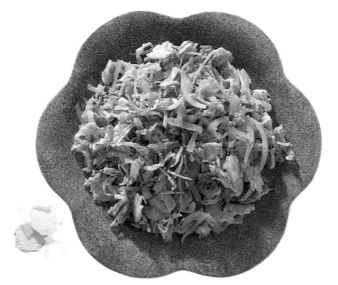

—GINGERED BRUSSEL SPROUTS—

2 tablespoons vegetable oil
1 onion, cut lengthwise in half and thinly sliced
1 or 2 garlic cloves, finely chopped
1-inch piece gingerroot, peeled and cut into julienne
  strips
2 pounds Brussels sprouts, trimmed and shredded
1 tablespoon chopped stem ginger in syrup
Salt and red (cayenne) pepper

Heat a wok until hot. Add oil and swirl to coat wok. Add onion, garlic and gingerroot and stir-fry 1 minute. Stir in shredded sprouts and stem ginger and stir-fry 2 or 3 minutes.

Add 2 tablespoons water and cook, covered, 2 or 3 minutes, stirring once or twice. Uncover and add 1 tablespoon water if sprouts seem too dry. Season with salt and cayenne.

Makes 4 to 6 servings.

SPICY CAULIFLOWER

1/4 cup whole blanched almonds
1 large cauliflower, separated into flowerets
1/4 cup butter
1 onion, finely chopped
1/2 teaspoon chili powder
1/2 teaspoon turmeric
3 or 4 tablespoons lemon juice
1/2 cup dried bread crumbs
Salt and freshly ground pepper

Heat a wok until hot. Add almonds and dry-fry over medium heat until browned on all sides. Remove to a plate and cool. Chop almonds coarsely; set aside.

Half-fill the wok with water and over high heat, bring to a boil. Add cauliflower and simmer 2 minutes. Drain and rinse; set aside. Wipe wok dry and return to heat. Add butter to wok and swirl until melted. Add onion, chili powder and turmeric and stir-fry 2 or 3 minutes or until softened.

Add cauliflower and lemon juice and stir-fry 3 or 4 minutes or until crisp-tender. Add bread crumbs and chopped almonds and toss until cauliflowerets are well coated. Serve hot.

Makes 4 to 6 servings.

BOMBAY POTATOES WITH PEAS

1/4 cup vegetable oil
1 onion, finely chopped
2 garlic cloves, finely chopped
1 teaspoon whole cumin seeds
1 teaspoon black mustard seeds
1 tablespoon curry powder
4 teaspoons ground cardamom
1 pound potatoes, cut into 1/2-inch pieces and cooked
    until tender
1 (10-oz.) package frozen green peas, thawed
1 or 2 tablespoons lemon juice
2 tablespoons chopped cilantro

Heat a wok until hot. Add oil and swirl to coat wok. Add onion and garlic and reduce heat to medium. Stir-fry 4 to 6 minutes or until onion is tender and golden. Add cumin seeds and mustard seeds and stir-fry 2 minutes or until seeds begin to pop. Stir in curry powder and cardamom and stir-fry 2 or 3 minutes.

Add potatoes and peas and stir-fry 2 or 3 minutes, tossing to coat with spice mixture. Add lemon juice and cilantro. Stir-fry until potatoes are hot, adding a little water if potatoes begin to stick. Serve hot.

Makes 4 to 6 servings.

— SWEET & SOUR VEGETABLES —

5 teaspoons cornstarch
1 (15-1/2-oz.) can pineapple chunks in juice, drained,
    juice reserved
3 or 4 tablespoons light brown sugar
1/3 cup cider vinegar
2 tablespoons soy sauce
2 tablespoons dry sherry or rice wine
1/4 cup ketchup
2 tablespoons vegetable oil
2 carrots, thinly sliced
1 fennel bulb, thinly sliced
1 red bell pepper, cut lengthwise in half and thinly
    sliced
6 ounces canned baby corn, rinsed
6 ounces snow peas
1 zucchini, thinly sliced

In a small bowl, dissolve cornstarch in reserved pineapple juice. Stir in sugar, vinegar, soy sauce, sherry and ketchup until combined; set aside.

Heat a wok until very hot. Add oil and swirl to coat wok. Add carrots, fennel and bell pepper and stir-fry 3 or 4 minutes or until carrots just begin to soften. Stir cornstarch mixture and stir into wok. Bring to a boil and stir until sauce bubbles and thickens. Add baby corn, snow peas and zucchini and simmer 1 or 2 minutes. Stir in reserved pineapple chunks and stir-fry 30 minutes.

Makes 4 servings.

GLAZED CARROTS

3 tablespoons vegetable oil
4 carrots, thinly sliced
1 fennel bulb, thinly sliced
6 ounces snow peas
4 to 6 green onions, cut into 1-inch pieces
1/2 cup orange juice
2 or 3 tablespoons orange liqueur (optional)
1 tablespoon brown sugar
1/2 teaspoon ground cinnamon
Grated peel of 1 orange, segments removed for garnish
2 tablespoons butter, cut into small pieces

Heat a wok until hot. Add oil and swirl to coat wok. Add carrots and stir-fry 3 minutes. Add fennel and snow peas and stir-fry 2 or 3 minutes until vegetables are crisp-tender. Remove to a bowl. Add green onions to oil remaining in wok and stir-fry 30 seconds. Add orange juice, orange liqueur if using, brown sugar, cinnamon and orange peel. Boil 2 or 3 minutes or until slightly thickened and reduced by about half.

Gradually stir in butter until a smooth sauce forms. Add reserved vegetables and toss to coat with sauce. Stir-fry 30 to 45 seconds until heated through. Add orange segments. Serve hot.

Makes 6 servings.

SAUTEED POTATOES

2 tablespoons olive oil
2 tablespoons butter
2 bacon slices, diced
1 onion, sliced
1 garlic clove, finely chopped
1 to 1-1/2 pounds russet potatoes, cooked, peeled and
  cut into 1/2-inch slices
1 tablespoon chopped fresh rosemary or thyme or 1
  teaspoon dried leaf rosemary or thyme
2 or 3 tablespoons balsamic vinegar or fruit-flavored
  vinegar
Salt and freshly ground pepper

Heat a wok until hot. Add oil and butter and swirl to coat wok. Add bacon and stir-fry 2 minutes or until crisp. Add onion and garlic and stir-fry 2 or 3 minutes or until browned and beginning to soften.

Add potatoes and rosemary and toss to combine. Cook over low heat 3 to 5 minutes, stirring occasionally until potatoes are browned and crisp. Season with salt and pepper. Serve hot.

Makes 6 servings.

-CREAMY CUCUMBERS & LEEKS-

2 tablespoons butter
1 cucumber, peeled, seeded and cut into strips
2 leeks, washed, cut into strips
1 garlic clove, finely chopped
3 or 4 tablespoons dry sherry or white wine
1/2 cup whipping cream
3 tablespoons chopped fresh dill
Salt and freshly ground pepper

Heat a wok until hot. Add butter and swirl until butter melts. Add cucumber, leeks and garlic and stir-fry 2 or 3 minutes or until cucumber begins to turn translucent. Add sherry and stir-fry 1 minute or until liquid evaporates.

Add cream and toss vegetables to combine. Stir-fry 1 or 2 minutes or until vegetables are crisp-tender. Stir in dill and season with salt and pepper. Serve hot.

Makes 4 to 6 servings.

GREEK-STYLE VEGETABLES

CHERRY TOMATO STIR-FRY

2 tablespoons olive oil
1 garlic clove, finely chopped
12 ounces red and yellow cherry tomatoes
4 green onions, thinly sliced
1/4 cup pine nuts or chopped hazelnuts, toasted
2 tablespoons chopped fresh basil plus herbs to garnish
1 tablespoon balsamic vinegar or red-wine vinegar
Freshly ground pepper

Heat a wok until hot. Add oil and swirl to coat wok. Add garlic and tomatoes and stir-fry 2 to 4 minutes or until tomato skins crinkle. Add onions, nuts, basil and vinegar. Stir-fry 1 minute; season and garnish.

BROAD BEANS GREEK STYLE

1-1/2 pounds broad beans or lima beans
2 tablespoons olive oil
1 garlic clove
1/2 teaspoon dried leaf oregano or basil
1/2 teaspoon sugar
1 teaspoon white-wine vinegar
1/2 cup crumbled feta cheese
Oregano leaves, to garnish

Place beans in wok and add enough water to cover. Bring to a boil and simmer 1 minute. Drain and rinse beans with cold water. Peel broad beans with your fingers.

Heat wok until hot. Add oil and swirl to coat wok. Add garlic and stir-fry 5 to 10 seconds, then remove and discard. Add beans, oregano and sugar and stir-fry 3 or 4 minutes over medium heat until beans are tender. Stir in vinegar. Remove from heat and toss with cheese. Garnish with oregano leaves and serve hot or warm.

Makes 4 servings.

-MEDITERRANEAN VEGETABLES-

ASPARAGUS WITH RADISHES
2 or 3 tablespoons olive oil
1-1/2 pounds asparagus, cut into 2-inch pieces
8 large radishes, thinly sliced
4 to 6 green onions, thinly sliced
2 tablespoons balsamic vinegar or cider vinegar
   (optional)

Heat wok until very hot. Add oil and swirl to coat wok. Add asparagus and stir-fry 2 or 3 minutes. Add radishes and onions and stir-fry 1 or 2 minutes or until asparagus is crisp-tender. Add vinegar if using and toss to coat.

ZUCCHINI WITH PROSCIUTTO
2 tablespoons vegetable oil
1-3/4 pounds zucchini, cut into thin strips
1 red bell pepper, cut into thin strips
1/4 cup light soy sauce
3 or 4 tablespoons rice vinegar or cider vinegar
1 tablespoon sesame oil
2 ounces sliced prosciutto, shredded
Chives, chopped

Heat a wok until hot. Add vegetable oil and swirl to coat wok. Add zucchini and bell pepper and stir-fry 3 or 4 minutes or until vegetables are crisp-tender. Stir in soy sauce, vinegar and brown sugar. Add sesame oil, prosciutto and chives. Toss to mix.

Makes 6 servings.

SPICY VEGETABLES

AROMATIC CABBAGE

1/4 cup vegetable oil
2 garlic cloves, finely chopped
2 tablespoons raisins
1 red bell pepper, very thinly sliced
1 teaspoon Chinese chili sauce
6 to 8 green onions, thinly sliced
2 or 3 tablespoons lemon juice
1 Chinese cabbage, thinly shredded

Heat a wok until hot. Add oil and swirl to
coat wok. Add garlic, raisins and bell pepper
and stir-fry 2 minutes. Stir in chili sauce,
green onions and lemon juice; toss. Add
cabbage and stir-fry 3 to 5 minutes.

ZUCCHINI WITH GINGER

2 tablespoons vegetable oil
2 or 3 garlic cloves
1-inch piece gingerroot, peeled and finely chopped
1/2 teaspoon chili powder
1 teaspoon sweet Chinese chili sauce or to taste
1/2 teaspoon sugar
1-1/2 pounds mixed green and yellow zucchini, cut into
   1-inch pieces

Heat a wok until hot. Add oil and swirl to
coat wok. Add garlic and gingerroot and stir-
fry 1 minute. Stir in chili powder, chili sauce
and sugar.

Add zucchini and toss to coat with flavorings.
Stir in 2 tablespoons water and stir-fry 3 to 5
minutes or until zucchini is crisp-tender,
adding more water if needed. Serve hot or at
room temperature.

Makes 6 servings.

—— WARM ANTIPASTI SALAD ——

Mixed salad leaves such as red leaf lettuce, radicchio
    and arugula
5 tablespoons olive oil
3 tablespoons red-wine vinegar or balsamic vinegar
1 (14-oz.) can artichoke hearts, drained and rinsed, cut
    in half if large
1 (8-oz.) can cannellini beans, drained and rinsed
1 garlic clove, chopped
1 red onion, chopped
1/2 teaspoon dried leaf basil
1 (7-oz.) jar roasted red bell peppers, drained and cut
    into 1/2-inch strips
4 sun-dried tomatoes, drained and cut into thin strips
1 tablespoon capers, drained and rinsed
1/2 cup Italian-style ripe olives

In a large bowl, toss salad leaves with 3 tablespoons of the oil and 2 tablespoons of the
vinegar. Arrange in a large shallow serving
dish. Heat a wok until hot. Add remaining
oil and swirl to coat wok. Add artichoke
hearts, beans, garlic, onion and basil and stir-
fry 2 or 3 minutes or until heated through.
Carefully spoon mixture over salad.

Add bell peppers and tomatoes to wok and
toss gently 1 or 2 minutes to heat through.
Arrange over salad. Sprinkle salad with
capers and olives and serve warm with crusty
bread.

Makes 4 to 6 servings.

WILTED SPINACH SALAD

1 pound spinach leaves, large stems removed
3 tablespoons olive oil
4 bacon slices, chopped
1 fennel bulb, thinly sliced
2 tablespoons cider vinegar
1 tablespoon Dijon-style mustard
1 teaspoon sugar
Freshly ground pepper

Arrange spinach leaves in a large bowl, tearing up any large leaves into bite-size pieces.

Heat a wok until hot. Add oil and swirl to coat wok. Add bacon and stir-fry 2 to 3 minutes or until bacon is just crisp. Add fennel and mushrooms and stir-fry 2 or 3 minutes until crisp-tender.

Add vinegar, mustard, sugar and pepper, tossing to coat vegetables. Pour over spinach leaves and turn leaves gently to coat; leaves will wilt at once. Serve immediately.

Makes 4 to 6 servings.

Variation: Garnish with lemon slices and radishes.

STIR-FRIED BEAN SALAD

6 ounces small green beans, cut into 2-inch pieces
6 ounces green runner beans, cut into 2-inch pieces
6 ounces snow peas
1/2 cup olive oil
1 onion, chopped
2 garlic cloves, finely chopped
1 (16-oz.) can red kidney beans, drained and rinsed
1 (15-oz.) can cannellini beans, drained and rinsed
1 (12-oz.) can whole-kernel corn, drained and rinsed
1/4 cup white-wine vinegar
2 tablespoons Dijon-style mustard
1 teaspoon sugar
1/2 pound sharp Cheddar cheese, diced
3 tablespoons chopped parsley

Half-fill a wok with water. Over high heat, bring to a boil. Add green beans and simmer 2 minutes. Add snow peas and bring back to a boil. Drain and rinse under cold water. Wipe wok dry and return to heat. Heat wok until hot. Add 2 or 3 tablespoons oil and swirl to coat wok. Add onion and garlic and stir-fry 3 minutes or until softened. Stir in kidney beans, cannellini beans and corn and stir-fry 3 minutes.

Add green beans and snow peas and stir-fry 3 minutes or until heated through. Remove from heat, turn into a large bowl and cool slightly. In a small bowl, whisk together vinegar, mustard and sugar. Whisk in remaining oil and pour over bean mixture. Add cheese and parsley and toss to mix. Serve warm or at room temperature.

Makes 6 servings.

—— PASTA PRIMAVERA ——

1 pound tagliatelle, linguine or thin spaghetti
2 to 4 tablespoons olive oil
8 ounces asparagus, cut into 2-inch pieces
8 ounces broccoli flowerets
2 yellow or green zucchini, sliced
4 ounces snow peas, cut in half if large
2 to 4 garlic cloves, finely chopped
1 (14-oz.) can chopped tomatoes
2 tablespoons butter
4 ounces fresh or frozen green peas
4 to 6 tablespoons shredded fresh basil
Shaved Parmesan cheese, to serve

In a large saucepan of boiling water, cook pasta according to package directions.

Drain pasta, turn into a large bowl and toss with 1 tablespoon of the oil. Heat a wok until hot. Add remaining oil and swirl to coat wok. Add asparagus and broccoli and stir-fry 4 minutes or until crisp-tender. Remove to the bowl with pasta. Add zucchini and snow peas and stir-fry 1 or 2 minutes or until crisp-tender. Remove to bowl. Add garlic to oil remaining in wok and stir-fry 1 minute. Stir in chopped tomatoes and their juice and simmer 4 to 6 minutes or until slightly thickened.

Stir butter into tomato sauce and add reserved pasta and vegetables and basil. Toss to coat well. Stir and toss 1 minute to heat through. Serve with Parmesan cheese.

Makes 6 servings.

— PENNE, VODKA & TOMATOES —

1 pound penne or rigatoni
2 tablespoons olive oil
1 onion, finely chopped
2 garlic cloves, finely chopped
1 (14-oz.) can plum tomatoes
1/2 teaspoon crushed dried chiles
4 ounces thinly sliced ham, cut into strips
1/2 cup vodka
1 cup whipping cream
1/2 cup grated Parmesan cheese
1/4 cup chopped parsley
Salt and freshly ground pepper

In a large saucepan of boiling water, cook pasta according to package directions.

Drain pasta and set aside. Heat a wok until hot. Add oil and swirl to coat wok. Add onion and garlic and stir-fry 2 minutes or until onion begins to soften. Add tomatoes and crushed chiles and bring to a boil. Reduce heat and simmer 10 minutes or until sauce thickens slightly.

Add ham and stir in vodka and simmer 5 minutes. Add cream and half of the cheese and simmer 3 minutes. Stir in pasta and parsley and toss to coat pasta. Season with salt and pepper and heat through. Serve with remaining cheese.

Makes 4 to 6 servings.

—MACARONI WITH EGGPLANT—

1 pound eggplant, cut into 1/4-inch strips
1 pound macaroni
3 tablespoons olive oil
3 garlic cloves, finely chopped
1 pound tomatoes, peeled, seeded and chopped
1 fresh hot red chile, seeded and chopped
4 ounces Italian salami, cut into julienne strips
1/2 cup Italian-style ripe olives
2 tablespoons capers, drained and rinsed
1/4 cup shredded fresh basil or oregano
1 cup crumbled feta cheese (4 oz.)
1/4 cup grated Parmesan cheese

Place eggplant strips into a colander and sprinkle with salt. Toss to mix and let stand, on a plate, 1 hour. Rinse with cold water and pat dry with paper towels.

In a large saucepan of boiling water, cook pasta according to package directions. Drain pasta and set aside. Heat a wok until very hot. Add oil and swirl to coat wok. Add eggplant and stir-fry 4 minutes or until browned. Drain on paper towels. Add garlic, tomatoes and chile and stir-fry 2 minutes or until juices are absorbed. Add salami, olives, capers, basil, eggplant and pasta and toss to coat well. Heat through. Stir in feta cheese and remove from heat. Serve with Parmesan cheese.

Makes 6 servings.

TORTELLONI SALAD

12 ounces cheese- or meat-filled spinach tortelloni
1/2 cup olive oil
2 garlic cloves, finely chopped
8 ounces asparagus, cut into 2-inch pieces
6 ounces broccoli, cut into small flowerets
1 yellow bell pepper, thinly sliced
1 (6-oz.) jar marinated artichoke hearts, drained
1 red onion, thinly sliced
2 tablespoons capers, drained and rinsed
1/4 cup Italian-style ripe olives
3 tablespoons red-wine vinegar
1 tablespoon Dijon-style mustard
Salt and freshly ground black pepper
3 tablespoons shredded fresh basil or parsley

In a large saucepan of boiling water, cook pasta according to package directions. Drain pasta, turn into a large bowl and toss with 1 tablespoon of the oil. Heat a wok until hot. Add 2 tablespoons oil and swirl to coat wok. Add garlic, asparagus and broccoli and stir-fry 4 minutes or until vegetables are crisp-tender. Add bell pepper and stir-fry 1 minute. Add vegetables to pasta and toss with artichoke hearts, onion, capers and olives. Cool to room temperature.

In a small bowl, whisk together vinegar, mustard, salt and pepper. Slowly whisk in remaining oil until creamy. Pour dressing over salad and toss gently to mix well. Serve at room temperature.

Makes 4 to 6 servings.

—PASTA WITH PEANUT SAUCE—

1 pound thin spaghetti
2 tablespoons sesame oil
8 ounces lean ground pork
1 red bell pepper, thinly sliced
4 ounces snow peas, cut diagonally in half
1 tablespoon sugar
1-inch piece gingerroot, grated
1/2 teaspoon crushed dried chiles
1/4 cup soy sauce
3 tablespoons cider vinegar
2/3 cup peanut butter
8 green onions, thinly sliced
2 tablespoons chopped cilantro

In a large saucepan of boiling water, cook pasta according to package directions. Drain pasta, turn into a large bowl and toss with 1 tablespoon of the oil. Place pork into a cold wok and cook over medium heat, stirring and breaking up meat, until pork is no longer pink. Add bell pepper, snow peas and sugar and stir-fry 1 minute. Add gingerroot, crushed chiles, soy sauce, vinegar, peanut butter and 2/3 cup hot water; cook, stirring, until sauce bubbles and peanut butter thins out. Add more water if needed.

Stir in green onions and reserved pasta. Toss and stir-fry 2 or 3 minutes until pasta is coated evenly with sauce and is heated through. Toss with cilantro.

Makes 4 to 6 servings.

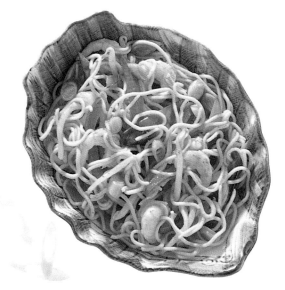

SINGAPORE NOODLES

8 ounces thin round noodles
1/4 cup vegetable oil
2 garlic cloves, chopped
1-inch piece gingerroot, peeled and finely chopped
1 fresh hot red chile, seeded and chopped
1 red bell pepper, thinly sliced
4 ounces snow peas, sliced if large
4 to 6 green onions, thinly sliced
6 ounces peeled cooked shrimp
4 ounces bean sprouts
1/3 cup ketchup
1 teaspoon chili powder
1 teaspoon Chinese chili sauce

In a large saucepan of boiling water, cook noodles according to package directions. Drain noodles, turn into a large bowl and toss with 1 tablespoon of the oil. Heat a wok until hot. Add remaining oil and swirl to coat wok. Add garlic, gingerroot and chile and stir-fry 1 minute. Add bell pepper and snow peas and stir-fry 1 minute.

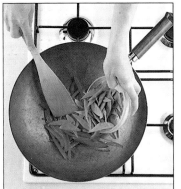

Add green onions, shrimp and bean sprouts. Stir in ketchup, chili powder, chili sauce and 1/2 cup water. Bring to a boil. Add noodles and stir-fry 2 minutes or until coated with sauce and heated through. Serve hot.

Makes 4 servings.

COCONUT NOODLES

8 ounces whole-wheat spaghetti or linguine
4 tablespoons peanut oil
4 ounces shiitake or oyster mushrooms, cut in halves
1 red bell pepper, thinly sliced
1/2 small Chinese cabbage, shredded
4 ounces snow peas, thinly sliced
4 to 6 green onions, thinly sliced
3/4 cup unsweetened coconut milk
2 tablespoons rice wine or dry sherry
1 tablespoon soy sauce
1 tablespoon oyster sauce
1 teaspoon Chinese chili sauce
1 tablespoon cornstarch dissolved in 2 tablespoons
   water
1/2 cup chopped fresh mint or cilantro
Mint sprig, to garnish

In a large saucepan of boiling water, cook pasta according to package directions. Drain pasta, turn into a large bowl and toss with 1 tablespoon of the oil. Heat a wok until hot. Add remaining oil and swirl to coat wok. Add mushrooms, bell pepper and cabbage and stir-fry 3 minutes or until vegetables begin to soften. Stir in noodles, snow peas and green onions; stir-fry 1 minute.

Slowly add coconut milk, wine, soy sauce, oyster sauce and chili sauce and bring to a simmer. Stir cornstarch mixture and, pushing ingredients to one side, add to wok. Stir to combine liquid ingredients, then stir in chopped mint. Stir-fry 3 minutes or until heated through. Garnish with mint.

Makes 4 servings.

COLD SPICY NOODLES

1 pound soba (buckwheat) noodles or whole-wheat
   spaghetti
2 tablespoons sesame oil
2 garlic cloves, finely chopped
1 green bell pepper, thinly sliced
4 ounces snow peas, sliced
4 ounces daikon, thinly sliced
2 tablespoons light soy sauce
1 tablespoon cider vinegar
1 or 2 tablespoons Chinese chili sauce
2 teaspoons sugar
1/3 cup peanut butter or sesame butter
8 to 10 green onions, thinly sliced
Chopped peanuts or sesame seeds, to garnish

In a large saucepan of boiling water, cook noodles according to package directions. Drain noodles, turn into a large bowl and toss with 1 tablespoon of the oil. Heat a wok until very hot. Add remaining oil and swirl to coat wok. Add garlic and stir-fry 5 to 10 seconds. Add bell pepper, snow peas and daikon. Stir-fry 1 minute until fragrant and peas are bright green.

Stir in soy sauce, vinegar, chili sauce, sugar, peanut butter and 1/4 cup hot water. Remove from heat and stir until peanut butter is smooth, adding more water if needed. Add reserved noodles and stir to combine. Turn into a bowl and cool. Stir in green onions and sprinkle with peanuts.

Makes 4 to 6 servings.

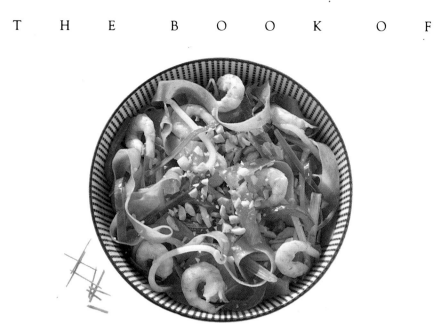

—— THAI RICE NOODLES ——

8 ounces flat rice noodles
3 tablespoons vegetable oil
2 garlic cloves, chopped
1 red bell pepper, thinly sliced
1 tablespoon soy sauce
1 teaspoon Chinese chili sauce
2 tablespoons nam pla (fish sauce)
4 teaspoons white-wine vinegar
1 tablespoon brown sugar
1 pound cooked peeled shrimp
6 ounces bean sprouts
6 green onions, thinly sliced
1/4 cup sesame oil
3 tablespoons chopped peanuts, to garnish

Place noodles into a large heatproof bowl. Add enough hot water to cover noodles by 2 inches and let stand 15 minutes or until softened. Drain and set aside. Heat a wok until very hot. Add vegetable oil and swirl to coat wok. Add garlic and bell pepper and stir-fry 3 minutes or until pepper is crisp-tender. Add noodles, soy sauce, chili sauce, nam pla, vinegar and sugar and stir-fry 1 minute. Add a little water if noodles begin to stick.

Stir in shrimp, bean sprouts, green onions and sesame oil and stir-fry 2 or 3 minutes until shrimp are hot. Sprinkle with peanuts and serve hot.

Makes 4 servings.

ASIAN-STYLE FRIED RICE

1-1/2 cups long-grain rice
3 tablespoons olive oil
2 garlic cloves, finely chopped
1/2-inch piece gingerroot, peeled and minced
2 tablespoons light soy sauce
1 teaspoon sugar
2 teaspoons nam pla (fish sauce)
1/2 teaspoon turmeric
4 to 6 green onions, thinly sliced
1 pound cooked peeled small shrimp
1 (8-oz.) can unsweetened pineapple chunks, juice
    reserved
3 tablespoons chopped cilantro

In a large saucepan of boiling water, cook rice about 15 minutes or until just tender. Drain in a colander and rinse with cold water. Set aside. Heat a wok until hot. Add oil and swirl to coat wok. Add garlic and gingerroot and stir-fry 1 minute. Add soy sauce, sugar, nam pla, turmeric and green onions, stirring to dissolve sugar.

Stir in reserved rice, the shrimp and pineapple, tossing to mix. Stir-fry about 4 minutes or until rice is heated through. Stir in some reserved pineapple juice if rice begins to stick. Stir in cilantro and serve hot.

Makes 4 to 6 servings.

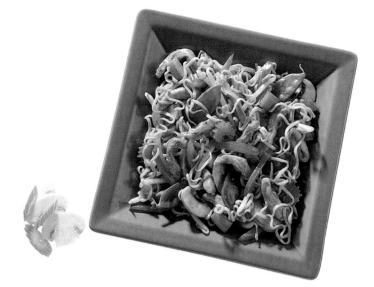

CHOW MEIN

3 tablespoons soy sauce
2 tablespoons dry sherry or rice wine
1 teaspoon Chinese chili sauce
1 tablespoon sesame oil
2 tablespoons cornstarch
12 ounces skinless boneless chicken breasts, shredded
8 ounces Chinese long noodles or linguine
2 tablespoons vegetable oil
2 celery stalks, thinly sliced
6 ounces button mushrooms
1 red or green bell pepper, thinly sliced
4 ounces snow peas
4 to 6 green onions, thinly sliced
1/2 cup chicken stock or water
4 ounces bean sprouts

In a shallow baking dish, combine soy sauce, sherry, chili sauce, sesame oil and cornstarch. Add chicken and stir to coat evenly. Let stand 20 minutes. In a large saucepan of boiling water, cook noodles according to package directions. Drain and set aside.

Heat a wok until hot. Add oil and swirl to coat wok. Add celery, mushrooms and bell pepper and stir-fry 3 minutes or until vegetables begin to soften. Add snow peas and green onions and stir-fry 1 minute. Remove to a bowl. Add chicken and marinade to oil remaining in wok. Stir-fry about 3 minutes or until chicken is no longer pink. Add stock and bring to a boil, then add reserved noodles and vegetables and bean sprouts. Stir-fry 2 minutes or until sauce thickens.

Makes 4 to 6 servings.

WOK-STYLE PAELLA

2 tablespoons olive oil
1 pound chorizo sausage or hot Italian sausage, cut into
    1-inch slices
1 pound skinless boneless chicken breasts, cut into
    1-inch slices
1 onion, chopped
2 or 3 garlic cloves, finely chopped
1 green or red bell pepper, diced
1 (14-oz.) can tomatoes
2-2/3 cups long-grain rice
1/2 teaspoon crushed dried chiles
1/2 teaspoon dried leaf thyme
1 teaspoon crushed saffron threads
8 ounces green beans, cut into 1-inch pieces
8 ounces cooked peeled shrimp (optional)

Heat a wok until hot. Add oil and swirl to coat wok. Add sausage and stir-fry 4 or 5 minutes or until golden. Remove to a plate. Add chicken to oil in wok and stir-fry 3 or 4 minutes or until golden. Remove to a plate.

Add onion, garlic and bell pepper to drippings in wok and stir-fry 3 or 4 minutes or until crisp-tender. Stir in tomatoes, rice, 2 cups water, crushed chiles, thyme and saffron. Bring to a boil, stir in sausage and reduce heat to low. Cover tightly and cook 20 minutes until liquid is absorbed and rice is tender. Stir in chicken and green beans and cook, covered, 5 to 7 minutes or until beans are crisp-tender. Add shrimp if using and fluff with a fork. Cook, uncovered, 2 or 3 minutes.

Makes 6 to 8 servings.

— BANANAS WITH RUM & LIME —

1/4 cup butter
1/4 cup packed light brown sugar
1/2 teaspoon ground cinnamon
4 bananas, cut into 1/2-inch pieces
1/3 cup light rum
Grated peel and juice of 1 lime or lemon
2 tablespoons chopped almonds
Shaved fresh coconut or toasted shredded coconut, to
    decorate

Heat a wok until hot. Add butter and swirl to melt and coat wok. Stir in sugar and cinnamon and cook 1 minute until sugar melts and mixture bubbles.

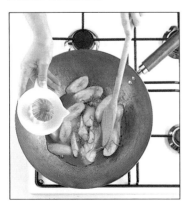

Add bananas and gently stir-fry 1 or 2 minutes, tossing to coat all pieces and heat through. Add rum and, with a match, ignite rum. Shake wok gently until flames subside. Add lime peel, lime juice and almonds. Spoon into dishes and top with coconut.

Makes 4 servings.

TOFFEE PEARS & PECANS

4 pears, peeled, cut in half lengthwise and cored
2 tablespoons lemon juice
5 tablespoons butter
1/2 cup packed brown sugar
'1 teaspoon ground cinnamon
1/2 teaspoon ground ginger
1 cup pecan halves
1 cup whipping cream
Vanilla extract

Cut pear halves into 1/4-inch-thick slices. Sprinkle with lemon juice.

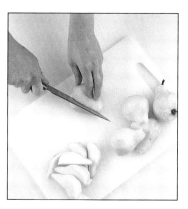

Heat a wok until hot. Add 2 tablespoons of the butter and 3 tablespoons of the brown sugar and swirl to coat wok. Stir until sugar melts and bubbles. Add pear slices, spices and pecans and stir-fry gently 4 to 6 minutes or until pear slices are crisp-tender. Remove pear mixture to a shallow serving dish.

Add remaining butter and sugar to wok and stir 2 minutes or until sugar dissolves and sauce boils. Stir in cream and bring to a boil. Simmer 3 minutes or until sauce thickens. Remove from heat, add a little vanilla and pour over pear mixture. Serve warm or at room temperature.

Makes 4 to 6 servings.

———— GINGERED FRUITS ————

8 ounces raspberries
2 tablespoons sugar
1 tablespoon lemon juice
1 or 2 tablespoons framboise (raspberry-flavored
 liqueur)
3 tablespoons butter
1 pound peaches or apricots, sliced
6 ounces apricots, sliced
2 or 3 plums, sliced
8 ounces black cherries, pitted
8 ounces seedless grapes
2 tablespoons chopped stem ginger in syrup
1/2 teaspoon ground ginger
4 ounces blueberries
Mint, to decorate
Yogurt or sour cream, to serve

In a blender or food processor, puree raspberries with sugar and lemon juice. Strain
through a sieve into a small bowl. Stir in
liqueur and a little water if needed to thin
sauce. Cover and refrigerate until ready to
serve. Heat wok until hot. Add butter and
swirl to melt and coat wok. Add peaches,
apricots and plums and stir-fry gently 3 or 4
minutes or until fruit just begins to soften.

Add cherries, grapes, stem ginger and ground
ginger. Stir-fry 2 or 3 minutes or until sliced
fruits are tender and cherries and grapes are
just heated through. Remove wok from heat
and stir in blueberries. Spoon fruit into a
serving dish and cool slightly. Drizzle with a
little raspberry sauce and pass remaining
sauce separately. Decorate with mint and
serve with yogurt.

Makes 6 to 8 servings.

MAPLE-GLAZED APPLES

1 lemon
4 Red Delicious apples, cut lengthwise and cored
1/4 cup butter
1-1/2 tablespoons light brown sugar
2 or 3 tablespoons maple syrup
1 teaspoon ground cinnamon
Whipping cream (optional)

With a vegetable peeler, remove yellow peel from lemon and cut into julienne strips.

Squeeze juice from lemon. Cut apple halves into 1/2-inch slices and sprinkle with lemon juice. Heat a wok until hot. Add butter, sugar, maple syrup and cinnamon and stir until sugar melts and sauce bubbles.

Add apple slices, lemon juice and lemon peel to sauce. Stir-fry gently 3 to 5 minutes or until apple slices just begin to feel tender and are glazed. Spoon into dessert dishes and drizzle with a little cream, if desired. Serve warm.

Makes 4 to 6 servings.

INDEX